"We're Only Postponing The Inevitable."

Alex shook his head. "We both know it. I want you in my bed, Stephanie, but when the time comes, I want to know it's through your choice and not because of the circumstances."

He leaned over and gave her a quick kiss. "I'll see you in a few hours for breakfast." Alex left her side and went into the other room, closing the door between them.

Stephanie couldn't believe what had almost happened. What Alex pointed out was going to happen...sooner or later.

She was in love with Colonel Alexander E. Sloan.

She must be out of her mind.

Dear Reader:

Happy Holidays to all of you!

This December brings not only three sensational books by familiar favorites—Jennifer Greene, Annette Broadrick and Sara Chance—but wonderful stories from a couple of newcomers: Jackie Merritt and Terry Lawrence. There's also a fabulous Christmas bonus, *'Tis the Season* by Noreen Brownlie, a novel full of the Christmas spirit about the best gift of all—the gift of love.

January marks the beginning of a very special new year, a twelve-month extravaganza with Silhouette Desire. We've declared 1989 the Year of the Man, and we're spotlighting one book each month as a tribute to the Silhouette Desire hero—our Man of the Month!

Created by your favorite authors, you'll find these men utterly irresistible. You'll be swept away by Diana Palmer's Mr. Janaury, (whom some might remember from a brief appearance in *Fit for a King*), and Joan Hohl's Mr. February is every woman's idea of the perfect Valentine....

Don't let these men get away!

Yours,

Isabel Swift
Senior Editor & Editorial Coordinator

ANNETTE BROADRICK
A Touch of Spring

Silhouette Desire

Published by Silhouette Books New York

America's Publisher of Contemporary Romance

SILHOUETTE BOOKS
300 East 42nd St., New York, N.Y. 10017

ISBN: 0-373-05464-5

First Silhouette Books printing December 1988

Printed in the U.S.A.

ANNETTE BROADRICK

lives on the shores of The Lake of the Ozarks in Missouri where she spends her time doing what she loves most—reading and writing romantic fiction. "For twenty-five years I lived in various large cities, working as a legal secretary, a very high-stress occupation. I never thought I was capable of making a career change at this point in my life, but thanks to Silhouette I am now able to write full-time in the peaceful surroundings that have turned my life into a dream come true."

To Candy, a valued friend,
with my love . . .

One

Stephanie Benson stared at the photograph lying faceup on her desk and knew that she was in trouble. The black-and-white glossy image of a man stared back at her intently. Big trouble.

She ran her hand through her hair, ignoring the fact that because of the action, her careful coiffure of early morning was now gone. She had considerably more to worry about than a tousled hairdo.

Stephanie studied the photograph carefully, hoping to find some softening in the features of Alexander Sloan that would reassure her that the next three and a half weeks in her life were not going to be difficult.

She could find no reassurance.

Colonel Sloan had not been wearing his air force uniform when the picture was taken. As a publicist, Stephanie already knew that the colonel could not wear his uniform nor have any photographs taken in uniform while he promoted his book.

However, his background and training in the military were evident. His unsmiling expression pointed out his strong jawline, but it did not detract from the sensual curve of his lips. His nose looked as though he'd been in at least one fight that hadn't gone his way. Stephanie found it was his eyes that caused the feeling of tension to creep over her.

Here was a man who would not be easily led through his paces while he traveled cross-country promoting his book.

Stephanie almost groaned out loud. So much for new experiences.

When Harry Mattingly, her boss, had called her into his office a few weeks ago, Stephanie had had no inkling of the bombshell he was preparing to drop on her.

She closed her eyes and leaned her head back against the comfortable executive chair she occupied. Good old Harry. Sooner or later she would learn not to trust that smile of his.

"How did the tour go?" he'd asked as soon as she sat down in front of him.

"Like all the rest, Harry," she admitted with a grin. "Organized chaos, as usual. Schedules that were almost impossible to meet, one lovesick author who had to be consoled each evening when her boyfriend wasn't home to answer her phone calls—you know, the usual."

Stephanie had been working as a publicist for almost five years, which automatically made her eligible for the Insanity Club. Who would ever choose to work with temperamental writers whose paranoia and trembling egos needed handling with utmost care? Even worse, she throve on it.

She adored the job. Perhaps it was because she enjoyed challenges, enjoyed creating order out of utter confusion. And perhaps it was because she had an overdeveloped case of the mother hen syndrome.

No doubt that had something to do with being the oldest child in a family of four; of having three younger brothers that she had herded into adulthood. Whatever the reason, Stephanie felt she had found her niche in the Mattingly Agency.

Harry seemed to think the same thing. For five years she had worked almost exclusively with women writers, many of whom wrote romantic fiction. She and her assistant had a routine lined up that worked very well. With enough lead time they could arrange multimedia coverage in every city she and the author visited.

Stephanie was good at what she did. Whatever Harry had in mind that morning, she knew she wasn't going to get any reprimands. The company had received nothing but excellent reports on the tour she had just completed. The publisher was happy, the authors were happy, the local people who had coordinated the appearances were happy. They had sold books, which was what her career was all about.

Stephanie crossed her long, well-shaped legs and waited to hear whatever it was Harry had called her into his office to say.

"I've got a new assignment for you," he said, glancing down at a file opened in front of him. "Have you ever heard of Alexander Sloan?"

The name sounded familiar, but she couldn't seem to place him. Slowly, she shook her head.

"Colonel Alexander Sloan has been assigned to the Pentagon for the past two years. Before that, he had spent most of his military time overseas."

Now Stephanie remembered where she had heard of him. "He's written a novel, hasn't he?" she asked.

Harry nodded. "That's right."

"There's speculation that it was based on some of his personal experiences."

"Speculation is all right, I suppose, if it sells books."

"You mean he didn't draw on his actual experiences?"

"Who knows? All I know is that his publisher wants us to arrange a tour for him to promote the novel. I want you to handle it."

"Me! But that's not my field."

"Look, Stephanie, you're one of the best publicists in the firm. You've got a cool head and work well under pressure. You're innovative and can handle the most temperamental clients. You're perfect for the job."

She looked at him suspiciously. "Oh, really? Are you trying to tell me that this Colonel Sloan is temperamental?"

"I wouldn't say that. Not exactly. It's just that his agent had some problem convincing Colonel Sloan that a tour would be what he needed to further his career.''

Stephanie rested her head briefly in her hand. ''Great. I suppose I'm to convince him of the need for publicity?''

''Nope. His agent finally did that. It just took him a while, or so I hear.'' Harry stood up and handed her the file. ''You'll need to get on this right away. The publisher has given us a list of seven cities to cover in ten days. That should keep you moving.''

''Seven cities! Come on, Harry. Let's be serious. Three cities in a week is hard enough. No one can keep going much longer than that.''

''I realize the schedule isn't easy, but this is an unusual case. The colonel has to take leave to be able to promote his novel. He says he can't take more time than that. The publisher is making the best use of the time Sloan is willing to give.''

Quickly thumbing through the file, Stephanie saw a biography, copies of early reviews of his novel and the photograph. She shrugged. ''Okay, Harry, I'll do my best.''

Harry smiled. ''Your best has always been more than satisfactory, my dear.'' His smile widened into a grin. ''Of course, Kent might not be too pleased. This will be the first time you've traveled with a man.''

Stephanie glanced at him in surprise. Harry should know better than anyone that she kept her professional and personal lives completely separate. So did Kent. ''If Kent and I didn't fully trust and believe in each other, Harry, we wouldn't be planning to marry this summer.'' Her steady gaze met his calmly.

He hastily agreed. "I know, I know. You and Kent are an ideal couple. I was just teasing you a little."

She smiled at his uncomfortable expression. "You have my permission to tease as much as you wish. You and Carleen practically adopted me when I moved here from California."

He grinned. "Someone needed to help you learn how to mingle with the natives."

"All I know is that I've enjoyed New York, love working for you and will take your irascible colonel on tour and mellow him with all of my charm and expertise."

"Great. Now get out of here so I can get some work done."

She looked down at the file again. "We're to begin May fifteenth. Is that right?"

"Yes. That should give you plenty of time to set up the tour."

She raised one eyebrow slightly. The first of March was rapidly approaching. Harry knew better than anyone else how long it took to plan a tour—to get the proper coverage, to make the necessary arrangements for public appearances. He was just trying to get a reaction out of her.

Stephanie gave him her most mischievous grin. "Of course it will. I'm sure the tour will go without a hitch...."

Now, almost two months later, Stephanie wasn't nearly so sure that her prediction had been accurate.

She opened her eyes and glanced down at the photograph in front of her once again. Colonel Alexander Sloan was proving to be less than cooperative, which was a new experience for her.

As a rule, all of the authors she had accompanied on tour had been not only willing but eager to promote their books, recognizing the worth of a tour. She had always found them to be friendly and receptive to her suggestions prior to the tours, even if they sometimes became fractious during the harrowing days of keeping up with the fast-paced schedules necessary.

Not so the elusive colonel. Stephanie had lost track of the number of calls she had made to the Pentagon in an effort to speak to Colonel Sloan. After going through some sort of mysterious chain of command, she invariably discovered that he was unable to take her call. Stephanie was always politely requested to leave a message if she wished.

Stephanie had left her name, her company's name and her phone number on several occasions, none of which had stirred the colonel enough to respond.

Consequently, the colonel's behavior had caused her to form a less than flattering opinion of the man.

She leaned her elbows on the desk and studied the picture once more. "Does that look intimidate people, Colonel Sloan?" she asked. "Do you find that you generally get your own way whenever you stare so intently at a person?"

Idly, she wondered what color his eyes were. They appeared to be light—either blue, green or gray. And in this particular photograph they came across as almost frosty. She wondered if he knew how to smile. Stephanie sincerely hoped so. It would make her job a heck of a lot easier.

She paused for a moment, remembering Harry's comments regarding her proposed tour with a male author and Kent's reaction. Stephanie had correctly guessed that Kent would take the trip in stride. After all, they had been seeing each other for almost four years. Both of them traveled extensively, both were serious about their careers and both were delighted to discover someone who understood their need for freedom without feeling threatened.

She and Kent had carefully weighed the threat of careers to a permanent relationship and had chosen to marry, knowing that their marriage would not be as close as some, but highly satisfying to their own special needs.

Stephanie glanced at her watch. As a matter of fact, Kent was due to arrive in town sometime today. He wasn't sure what flight he'd be on, but had promised to call her when he got in. She was looking forward to spending a relaxing evening with him, hearing about his trip, and telling him about the events she had experienced since he had gone.

Resolutely, she reached for the phone to attempt to contact dear Colonel Sloan once more. Despite the amount of work she had to do, she had almost memorized the phone number to the Pentagon. Perhaps today she would be lucky.

After a considerable wait, she finally reached her elusive client.

"Colonel Sloan," said a deep voice that caught her off guard for a moment. Stephanie had been prepared to leave yet another message.

Quickly, she glanced down at the paper in front of her.

"Good morning, Colonel Sloan, this is Stephanie Benson."

"Yes?"

There was no sign of recognition of her name. "With the Mattingly Agency," she added, hoping to prod his memory.

"Is this some sort of solicitation, Ms. Benson? You've certainly been persistent, I'll give you that. However, I don't think—"

"This is *not* a solicitation, Colonel! I am your publicist."

There was a brief pause, then a very quiet voice asked, "My what?"

"I am in charge of the tour promoting your novel, Colonel. Didn't your agent tell you?"

The pause was longer this time. Finally, he spoke. "I thought the tour had been canceled."

Stephanie paused for a deep breath and prayed for patience. "Why would you think that?"

"Because no one has gotten in touch with me about it, for one thing."

"Not for lack of trying, Colonel," she replied dryly.

"I see," he said thoughtfully.

"As a matter of fact, we are to begin in Philadelphia in two weeks. We'll meet at the airport on Sunday evening, May fifteenth."

"I'm sorry, but I'm afraid I can't make it then. Perhaps a little later."

Stephanie began to count to ten, very slowly. Then she waited a few more seconds to ensure that her tone of voice was warm and cordial before she replied.

"Colonel Sloan, perhaps you don't understand exactly what is involved. I have spent over two months arranging this tour. We've got seven cities to cover in ten days. Your agent and your publisher have both assured us that you are willing to promote this novel and we have worked on that assumption."

"But that's only a couple of weeks away and I've made other arrangements for that weekend," he replied.

"Perhaps your other arrangements could be postponed until your return, once you explain the circumstances," she suggested politely.

Stephanie tried to keep her tone level and unemotional, but she wasn't at all sure she had succeeded. What an exasperating man. She glared at the photograph lying in front of her, feeling a certain sense of satisfaction at venting that much of her irritation toward him.

"I suppose that is possible, Ms.—uh—Benson," he replied. "I just wish that I had been notified that the tour was planned to begin May fifteenth."

"Believe me, Colonel Sloan. I did everything I could to get that information to you. I sent several letters. When you didn't respond, I thought I might not have your correct address, so I began to call you. Perhaps if you would have returned any one of my phone calls..." she pointed out in a reasonable tone of voice.

"Yes, I can certainly see your point." She was surprised to hear a note of amusement creep into his voice. "I feel certain you are most efficient and have everything well organized," he added smoothly.

Why did she get a distinct feeling he was being sarcastic?

No matter. Now that she had his attention she would go over the details. For the next several minutes she explained some of the major points arranged for the tour. By the time they were through, he was fully conversant with his role for the upcoming weeks. After verifying that she did in fact have his correct address, Stephanie ended the conversation by saying, "I will send you a copy of our itinerary so that you can give it to your family or office in case anyone needs to contact you while you're away."

"That will be helpful, I'm sure," he agreed in a bland tone of voice.

She tried to ignore her reaction to his patronizing attitude and continued. "I think that covers everything," she said. "I will be looking forward to meeting you, Colonel Sloan, at the airport in Philadelphia on the fifteenth."

"How will I know you?" he asked.

"I have your photograph, Colonel, and I'm sure I'll recognize you. Will you be in uniform?"

"No. I'll be taking my leave to go on tour. My military life needs to be kept totally separate from my novel."

"That's going to be a little difficult to accomplish. Everyone knows that your military background has a great deal to do with the subject matter of your book."

"Oh, do they?" he asked with deceptive politeness. "How interesting. I should have realized that one can't fool the public these days."

Stephanie couldn't fault the politeness of his tone but was more than convinced that his comments were not as straightforward as he wanted them to appear.

This was one tour she was not looking forward to making. Something told her the colonel was going to be a much different author to deal with than the writers she had accompanied in the past.

"Thank you for your time, Colonel," she said politely.

"My pleasure, Ms. Benson," he said, equally polite.

When Stephanie hung up the phone, she immediately closed Alexander Sloan's file and placed it to one side of her desk. She'd had as much of him in one dose as she was willing to handle.

Stephanie forced herself not to think about the ten days that would throw her into his constant company. She would deal with him professionally, she knew. In the meantime she had a great deal to do for other clients before she left for Philadelphia.

Alex Sloan absently stared at the phone for several minutes after he hung up. So the publicist for his tour was a woman. Stephanie Benson.

When his agent, Samuel Hendricks, had discussed the possibility of a tour, Alex had not given the idea much thought. The whole subject of his book and its recent publication had been pushed to the back of his mind. He'd had no choice but to write the book. The story had drifted around inside his head for years, insisting on being told, until he could no longer ignore it. He had written it, and for all practical purposes, after finding an agent and turning it over to him, he'd forgotten it. Alex had no idea that once written the book would be so well received.

He had found a certain amount of relief in the routine of writing at night. Writing had become an escape from his daily life, an opportunity for him to express the emotions that he had been forced to keep locked away inside of him. He had seen so much. Too much. He'd witnessed enough nightmares to keep him awake for the rest of his life. Except these had been living nightmares, when he had been forced to witness the deaths of some of his closest friends; when he'd had to listen to Steve beg him to put him out of his misery.

Thank God Steve was doing better now. He'd decided to help in his own rehabilitation. Alex had told his friend that he'd spend the weekend of the fifteenth with him. Now he'd have to change his plans.

Once he'd finished his first book, Alex had started a second one, one not quite so painful, one where he could distance himself a little more. He enjoyed writing. Now that he was back in Washington, he much preferred spending his evenings writing, rather than becoming involved in the Washington social scene.

Joanne, his former wife, had never minced words about his lack of social graces. Alex preferred his own company most of the time, which was only one of the reasons Joanne had left him. She hadn't cared for the military life, the foreign assignments or the constant moves.

Alex had discovered a definite sense of relief when she decided, after several years of complaining, to divorce him. There was such a small part of his life that he was allowed to share with her. He returned home for relief from all that he encountered on his classified missions. Joanne soon grew tired of trying to show interest in what he did because of his deliberately vague answers. He was even worse at trying to show interest in her daily routines.

He had loved her at one time; he was sure of it. Just as he was sure that she had loved him. But too many separations over the years had seemed to emphasize the basic difference in their personalities. She enjoyed people, while he seemed inundated by them, feeling inadequate to fill their needs.

Her idea of a quiet, relaxing evening was to attend a social function somewhere, when all he wanted was to be quiet and to rest his jangled nerves.

They were both happier now. She had remarried and now had two children. He had been afraid of bringing a child into the world until his job became less dangerous. He wanted the opportunity to be a real father to a child—not just a picture of a man in a uniform hanging on the wall. Now it was too late for a family. It was almost ironic. So many of the men who had been there beside him—and died—had left families. He—who had no one—had come through it, visibly unscathed.

He carried his wounds inside of him.

Alex enjoyed feminine companionship from time to time. He knew several women whose company he had enjoyed in the years since his divorce. However, he had already learned a very valuable lesson. He had no intention of becoming attached to anyone again. Alex didn't want to endure the pain of losing them, whether through a physical death, or the death of their love for each other.

Alex idly wondered if Stephanie Benson was married. If she was, how did her husband feel about her traveling with another man?

Alex tried to place himself in that position and recognized that he'd been alone too long to guess. Joanne had never enjoyed going anywhere without an escort. Since Joanne, the women he'd dated had seemed content with their single lives, enjoying their independence. He couldn't imagine himself waiting at home for a wife to return from a business trip. He smiled to himself. He'd probably forget who she was by that time, he was so used to being on his own.

He wondered what Stephanie Benson looked like, how old she was and what sort of a traveling companion she would make. He would find out soon enough.

Alex picked up the pile of mail his secretary had placed before him. He had enough to do to clear his desk within two weeks. He grinned at the memory of her pointing out that it was his own fault. Indeed, it was.

Once again he had unofficially been out of the country and away from what was supposed to be his job. He couldn't very well tell her the truth since he went through an inordinate amount of trouble to give the impression he still came into his office daily. Thank God there were dependable people to cover for him.

The fact was that he had totally forgotten about the proposed tour. He wished Sam had called to remind him. He'd seen Stephanie's messages when he finally got to his office that morning, but he hadn't recognized her name. Other messages had practically screamed their urgency and he had postponed calling her.

He looked at his calendar, studying it with dismay. The delicate negotiations he was involved in were too important to be set aside for a tour. He was thankful that nothing was scheduled until the end of the month.

Seeing Steve was the only problem he had to work out. Maybe he'd go down to visit him this weekend and tease him about having to promote the book. After all, it was dedicated to Steve. He'd have to give him a bad time about Steve's prospective notoriety. Alex would do whatever it took to get a smile back on Steve's face and a sparkle in his eyes once more.

Too bad he couldn't fill him in on the prospect of traveling with a woman publicist. Perhaps they could lay bets on what she was like. He'd be willing to try most anything to get Steve on the road to recovery.

When Stephanie's secretary buzzed her several hours later, her mind was still on her work. Absently, she picked up the phone. "Yes?"

"Kent—on line two."

She smiled and answered the other line. "Welcome home, stranger. When did you get in?"

A warm male voice responded. "I'm standing here with my briefcase still in my other hand. Have you missed me?"

"Without a doubt."

"Good. Then I won't have to bribe you to have dinner with me tonight."

She laughed. "Have you ever? I'm a sucker for a free meal. You know that."

"I'm crushed. I thought it was me you were so eager to see."

"It is. Believe me, it is."

There was a silence for a moment, as though Kent was hesitating before saying something. Stephanie decided it must be her imagination. One of the greatest things about their relationship was the fact that they were so open with each other. She must have imagined the hesitation, because when he spoke he sounded very natural.

"I'll pick you up at seven. You can decide where we eat."

"You are such a trusting soul. No wonder I'm in love with you."

He didn't laugh at her teasing, but then she knew he must be tired after his trip.

"I'll see you at seven. I love you," she repeated.

"I love you, too, Stephanie," he said quietly.

"Laura? I'm home," Stephanie called out when she got inside their shared apartment.

Her roommate stuck her head out of the bathroom. "I suppose you need to get in here right away."

"Not necessarily. Why?"

"Oh, I decided to put an oil treatment on my hair."

"How exciting. I take it you don't have a date to-night."

Once more Laura stuck her head out the door. "You must have me confused with someone else, love."

Stephanie laughed. "Don't give me that. Other people might buy that tough exterior of yours. I know better."

"At least the men all seem to buy it. I've played career woman for so long that they don't even consider finding out if I'd like to have a personal life as well," Laura said from the other room. "Did you hear from Kent?"

Stephanie smiled, thinking about the call. She was glad to know he was back in town. "Yes. He'll be here at seven."

"Okay. I'll be out of your way in a few minutes."

"I've got plenty of time." She slipped on her robe and stretched out on the bed, pleased to have a few minutes to relax. "I finally got in touch with Colonel Sloan today," she said with a touch of pride in her voice.

Laura walked into the room with a towel wrapped around her head. A petite brunette, Laura exuded confidence and authority. Stephanie was never sure how she managed to do that. It must be something in the genes. "No kidding," Laura was saying. "Here I thought he was a figment of somebody's imagination, that Alexander E. Sloan didn't exist."

Stephanie smiled. "Believe me, I was beginning to think the same thing. No matter what time I called, I had always just missed him—and he'd never bother to return my calls."

"Did he say why?"

Stephanie thought about that for a moment. "Not really. He was charmingly pleasant... said he'd forgotten about the tour."

"Forgotten! How could he forget something as important as a national tour promoting his first novel? Does he have any idea how many authors there are who would kill for that sort of promotion by their publisher?"

"Obviously not," Stephanie responded dryly. "Or doesn't care. He seemed a little preoccupied through most of the conversation, as though I were a distraction."

Her roommate looked at Stephanie with a knowing smile. "If he could see you now, he would definitely find you a distraction."

Stephanie glanced down at the thin peach-colored robe she wore and shrugged. "I don't think you have to worry about him ever seeing me like this."

Laura shook her head, amused at her roommate's lack of vanity. Stephanie had the clear, porcelainlike complexion that cosmetic companies touted in their ads. Her silver-blond hair and translucent blue eyes caused double takes wherever she went, yet Stephanie seemed totally unaware of the impact she had on other people.

Laura knew that Stephanie was content with her life—her career, Kent and their upcoming marriage. Colonel Sloan might have to eat his heart out if he was as susceptible to beauty, intelligence and a charming personality as the next man. From what she had heard about him, he deserved to be knocked off base a little. Laura almost wished she could be a witness to their first meeting.

Several hours later Kent and Stephanie arrived at Kent's apartment for a chance to talk privately. Summer was rapidly approaching, and they hadn't set a definite date for the wedding. With their hectic schedules, Kent had once laughingly said they would just have to grab a license and a judge on the rare occasion when they were both in town at the same time.

Stephanie sank into the corner of Kent's sofa with a sigh. "I know you're tired, Kent. There was no reason for you to prolong your day with dinner tonight. We've got the weekend coming up, you know."

"I know," he said. "But we need to talk."

Kent handed her a glass of wine and sat down beside her. He was acting so unlike himself that he was beginning to make her nervous. One of the things about Kent that she most enjoyed was his ability to leave his business and come to her with a relaxed, wholehearted attitude. As much as he enjoyed what he did, he was willing to let go of it. And yet tonight he seemed preoccupied somehow. Whenever she asked if there was something on his mind, he would hastily deny it and change the subject. But there seemed to be something wrong. Stephanie wished she knew what it was.

Kent leaned over and kissed her. She enjoyed his kisses. They were warm and friendly. They were comfortable. Stephanie had no desire for the burning, passionate affairs that other women discussed from time to time. She didn't believe in them. They had no lasting value. Stephanie preferred a relationship built first on friendship and respect and mutual interests.

When Kent finally pulled away from her, she smiled softly at him. Her hand traced his jawline, and her forefinger traced his lips. "I've missed you," she whispered.

His dark eyes flashed for a moment. "Stephanie—" he began, and she heard a note of uncertainty in his voice she'd never heard before.

"There is something wrong, isn't there?" she asked.

"I don't know. I'm so confused at the moment that I don't know what I think about anything."

"Are you talking about us?"

"I wish I knew! I love you, Stephanie. I love everything about you—your warmth, your generous spirit, your loving nature, your beauty, both inside and out..."

"Why is it that I hear the unspoken word *but* hanging in the air, waiting to enter the conversation?"

He took her hand and turned it palm upward. Slowly, he began to trace the lines on her hand. "You and I have always been friends. We were friends long before we started dating, remember?"

She nodded, waiting for something that she was sure she didn't want to hear, but somehow knowing it was necessary.

"I need a friend," he said quietly.

She turned her hand over so that it clasped his. "You've got one."

"I don't want to hurt you."

"I know you don't. Just tell me. Whatever it is, go ahead and tell me."

He turned his head so that she faced his profile. Whatever he had to tell her was as painful for him to say as it was for her to hear. "As you know, Susan Powell and I have worked together for a couple of years now. We work well together." He stopped, glanced at her, then away.

For a brief moment Stephanie thought that she had gone numb. Her breathing seemed to have stopped, as well as her heart. This was bad, much worse than what she had thought he might have to say. This was attacking the very fabric of their relationship. And all she could do was to sit there...as a friend...and listen.

"We had a tough presentation to make this past week. We'd spent hours preparing it. The day we delivered it, we'd been up since five in the morning, and we were delirious when it was so well received."

"I know. You sounded ecstatic when you called," she said quietly.

He squeezed her hand, his eyes never quite meeting hers. "Yes. We'd forgotten to eat, so we had room service deliver a meal to the suite we were staying in." Once again he glanced around at her. "We always travel that way, you know, so that we have an extra room to work in and are close enough to stay in touch."

"Yes," she said faintly.

"We ordered champagne. We were both so excited that we were laughing and talking at the same time. I don't remember eating, or even drinking that blasted champagne. Sometime, though, we began to talk about how we had done it, how well we got along, how well we worked together.'' He got up and walked over to the window and looked out. With his back to the room he continued. "Then Susan told me that she was in love with me and had been since shortly after joining the firm."

Stephanie realized that she was shredding the fine linen handkerchief in her hands. "So you made love to her," she said softly.

Kent whirled from the window. "No! Of course not! I—well...uh...no. I'll admit that I kissed her. I have no excuse. None whatsoever. But I did not make love to her. In fact, I apologized, and she apologized for her confession, as she called it, and we ended up going to our separate rooms."

He began to pace the floor. "The thing is, I can't forget what she said, and what almost happened. I love you, I'm engaged to marry you, and yet there's something between Susan and me that—" He stopped and looked at her, bewildered. "I can't seem to put it out of my mind. I can't explain it. I just know that I can't sit here and blithely plan our marriage when I can't seem to get another woman out of my head."

Stephanie sat quietly for a moment, studying her hands, which lay in her lap. She knew she needed to say something, but her mind was blank. What could she say? Finally she glanced up. "I appreciate your honesty, Kent. I know it wasn't easy for you to tell me."

He came over to her and sat down beside her. "No, it wasn't. I don't want to hurt you, either now or later."

"So what do you want to do now?"

"I wish I knew! I've never had this happen to me before. I've known Susan all of this time and never saw her as anything but a business associate. Now—all at once—I can't stop thinking about her. I fantasize about her. I—oh, hell. You don't need to hear all of this."

He came over and sat down beside Stephanie. "God, I'm sorry, Steph. I must be losing my mind."

Quietly, Stephanie slipped off the engagement ring that Kent had given her for Christmas and laid it on the table in front of her. "Thank you for being honest with me. It's better to face this now than—" her voice wobbled slightly and she cleared her throat "—later."

He looked at the ring lying in front of them and shook his head. "I can't believe what's happening." Slowly, he turned his head until his eyes met hers. They each saw the pain in the other's eyes. "I'm too young to be having a midlife crisis, don't you think?" he asked whimsically, in an attempt to lighten the atmosphere.

"I'm afraid I don't have any of the answers, Kent. However, I don't think either one of us needs any more of this discussion at the moment, do you?"

He shook his head and stood. "I'll take you home."

Neither one of them said anything until they reached her door. Stephanie blessed the state of numbness that seemed to surround her.

Kent waited until she unlocked her apartment door. Then he brushed his knuckles against her cheek. "I'll call you tomorrow, okay?"

Stephanie nodded, unable to say a thing. What did it matter whether he called or didn't? It was over, and both of them knew it.

Two

Stephanie sat in the waiting area of the Philadelphia airport, resigned to the fact that Colonel Sloan's plane was delayed once again.

Laura had spent the past two weeks trying to convince her to have Harry send someone else on this tour, but Stephanie had insisted on sticking with the original plans. She had to get on with her life and not waste her time on regrets. Sitting at home feeling sorry for herself would accomplish nothing. She refused to wallow in self-pity.

After all, this was no great tragedy she was going through, she kept reminding herself. It happened all the time. People fell in and out of love on a regular basis. The circumstances weren't all that unusual.

Kent's being so up-front about it was what had made their situation different. Many men would have refused to face the possibility of a distasteful scene. He could have broken the engagement without telling her why, or he could have made up some story, not caring whether or not she believed it. He also could have gone ahead and married her, continued to work with Susan and let whatever was going to happen between them happen, disregarding the possible consequences.

He had done none of those things. He had been honest enough to share with her exactly what was happening to him. However, the sharing hadn't made it any easier on either one of them.

She had not only lost a fiancé, she had lost a friend. A good friend. One who had been there for her so often, just as she had been there for him.

In the two weeks since he'd told her, they had spoken on the phone a few times, trying to save what they could of the relationship. Stephanie felt the attempted casualness of the calls had been just as painful as anything she had gone through.

She had come to face the fact that it takes more than common interests and a liking for each other to create the necessary bonds for a successful marriage. There had been a spark missing between her and Kent, one she had never wanted, one that he must have felt necessary. Whether or not he would find it with Susan was no longer any of her business.

She could have tried to convince him that he was merely flattered by the idea that Susan loved him, but what good would that have done? And what was going to happen if and when he decided that his feelings for

Susan weren't any more than a temporary aberration?

Whatever happened, there could never be the relationship they had originally hoped for. Trust was such a fragile thing and yet so crucial to a relationship. Although Stephanie still trusted Kent, she no longer trusted his emotions.

Nor could she trust her own. She knew that if they attempted to work through what had happened, she would always wonder who he was with when he was traveling, or if he was with Susan, what they were doing.

Trust. Such a small word for such an enormous responsibility in any relationship.

Stephanie wasn't certain that she would ever be able to share it with anyone again.

When Alex stepped off the plane and joined the milling crowd at the Philadelphia airport, he was more than mildly irritated. He'd been putting in long hours trying to catch up with paperwork that had stacked up while he'd been away, as well as trying to make sure things were covered during the next ten days. The tour couldn't have come at a worse time for him.

He was short of sleep and patience as he stood there, wondering who the hell he was looking for. All he wanted was to get checked into his hotel, have a couple of drinks to relax, and get some sleep. Instead, according to the itinerary his very efficient publicist had sent him, he was already overdue for a damned interview with the local press.

He glanced around impatiently. In a crowd this size he could be left standing around indefinitely. Why hadn't they agreed to meet at the hotel? He should have thought of that. The truth was that he had given very little thought to this trip, and now he was going to have to pay for it by relying on someone else to take the lead. Alex was used to taking command of situations and dealing with them. However, this time he was way out of his league. The realization didn't do anything positive for his frame of mind.

He heard his name from somewhere behind him. Turning around, he couldn't control the start of surprise he felt.

The woman standing before him had silver-blond hair and unforgettable blue eyes surrounded by thick lashes. Add to that a pert, slightly tilted nose, and a mouth that appeared to be made for kissing, and Alex suddenly felt that he'd walked into another dimension.

She looked nothing like the many variations that he and Steve had come up with the evening before. He'd been pleased to see Steve get into the mood by suggesting his publicist would be a tough, older woman wearing orthopedic shoes, her hair in a no-nonsense bun. Alex's version hadn't been much better, but admittedly he'd been going for laughs rather than actually trying to visualize Stephanie Benson.

Bemused, he found himself nodding his head in acknowledgment of her greeting as she stood before him, waiting for a response. "You must be Stephanie Benson," he finally said. He sensed a rather fragile air about her. He couldn't quite put his finger on what gave him that impression. There seemed to be a trace of sadness in the depths of her eyes, and yet they seemed so clear and candid that he felt as though he were peering into her soul while she steadily returned his gaze. He was impressed with the way her mauve suit set off her feminine shape. His gaze paused on her shapely legs, then met her eyes once more. He took the hand she offered him so professionally. "I'm very pleased to meet you," he added sincerely.

Stephanie had recognized him as soon as he had appeared, but it had taken her a few moments to adjust to the reality of Alexander E. Sloan. Not that the picture had created a false impression. It just hadn't done the man justice. The photograph had not shown his height or how his military posture emphasized his broad shoulders, narrow waist and muscled frame.

From his expression when he appeared, she knew he was going to be a difficult author to work with. He didn't look as though he particularly enjoyed following other people's instructions and suggestions.

Perhaps Laura had been right. Stephanie should have let someone else take this tour; someone who wasn't trying to come to terms with a future that had suddenly blown up in her face. Given time, Stephanie was confident she would be able to cope with all of the sudden changes. But not just yet. And Colonel Sloan appeared to be quite an obstacle to overcome in her journey.

Standing this close to the man, she realized that his eyes were a slate-gray, but contrary to the photograph there was nothing cold about them. In fact, the warmth and interest in them caused her to shiver briefly. He wasn't looking at her as his publicist. The all-encompassing perusal was definitely cataloging all of her feminine assets.

This is going to be the longest ten days I've ever spent, she thought faintly.

Trying to look at the more positive side, she realized that Colonel Sloan was going to make a great hit on the tour. Once the women saw him in person, they would be rushing to buy his book in order to have him autograph it.

Stephanie admitted that she couldn't really blame them. But then, they didn't have to travel with him, either. She wondered what Laura would think about that complaint.

Laura was of the opinion that one man was as good as the next. They were to be enjoyed, but never taken too seriously, and never, under any circumstances, were they to be relied on for more than occasional companionship. In fact, when she realized that she couldn't talk Stephanie into getting someone else to cover the tour, Laura suggested that she use the time to have a nice fling with the man in order to get Kent out of her system.

There were times when Stephanie wished she had Laura's rather unorthodox and singular approach to life. However, Stephanie knew there was no way she was going to get involved with a client, even if she was in the mood. Which she wasn't. She just wished the kind colonel would get that speculative gleam out of his eyes.

"Welcome to Philadelphia, Colonel Sloan," she finally said in the lingering silence that had fallen upon them after their first greeting. It wasn't particularly original or scintillating, but it certainly was an improvement over standing there with her mouth slightly agape, taking in the man's obvious sex appeal.

He gave her a lopsided smile that she found very endearing. The smile made him look several years younger. She wondered if he had any idea how attractive he was. Somehow she doubted it. He appeared to be unconscious of his effect on the people around him.

"Call me Alex," he said. "From the looks of our schedule we might as well get on a first-name basis, don't you think?"

Stephanie forced herself to stop staring at him and removed her hand from his grasp. "Of course." She looked around her as though unsure of what to do next. "Shall we go claim your luggage?" Stephanie suggested, forcing herself to treat him as she would any other client. *It's not him. It's just that you're so vulnerable at the moment,* she reminded herself. *Your ego has just taken a rather strong stomping, not to mention the ragged condition of your emotions.*

Despite all that had happened, Stephanie realized that her feelings for Kent had not really changed. She loved him. She just had to get used to the idea that despite that love, she would never marry him. Knowing that all of her hopes and dreams had suddenly gone up in smoke, it was probably natural that her imagination should immediately try to find someone else to fulfill her fantasies regarding love and marriage.

Surely, the fact that she acknowledged the tendency would help her from falling victim to it. She understood, therefore she could deal with her rather untrustworthy emotions and reactions.

She hoped.

Stephanie turned away from him and began walking down the concourse. Alex joined her and companionably took her arm.

Glancing down at her with a smile, he said, "You don't look at all like my idea of a publicist."

Stephanie felt herself stiffen and forced herself to reply in a noncommittal tone. "I'm not sure what you expected. Publicists can come in all shapes and sizes."

He studied the professional-looking woman walking beside him with more than a little curiosity. What had he said to cause the slight irritation he detected in her brusque tone? He thought he'd been paying her a compliment. For whatever reason, she hadn't chosen to accept it as such.

Not certain whether he was being brave or merely foolhardy, Alex chose to pursue the subject. "You're younger than I expected," he said, guiding her down the concourse in his usual long-limbed stride.

Stephanie found herself quickening her pace to keep up. "Looks can be deceiving," she muttered, so that he almost didn't hear her. Alex decided he wasn't going to win any points by pursuing that subject, so he said nothing more for the moment.

She did look young, though. She made him feel all of his forty-three years. He was probably old enough to be her father, although his reactions to her were anything but paternal.

You're tired, Sloan. Don't let your fantasies run away with you. He wished he could have requested a man on the trip, and grinned at the thought. He would have had every feminist in the country angry with him. It wasn't her competency he questioned, though. It was his own vulnerability. He hadn't been around a woman in quite a while, particularly one as attractive as Stephanie Benson. He'd really have to watch himself, or his agent and publisher would be on him like an avalanche in the Alps.

By the time they arrived at the baggage claim area, Stephanie noticed that she was out of breath. Her breathlessness had nothing to do with her reaction to the man whose hand still had a steady grip on her elbow. His long legs had caused her to almost run to keep up with him, that was all.

Alex glanced down at his watch and said, "We're already late for that interview. What do you suggest we do now?"

Stephanie was surprised that he remembered. His earlier cavalier attitude toward the tour had caused her to suppose he would not pay much attention to their itinerary. She was pleasantly surprised to discover that the colonel appeared to be ready to devote his attention and energies to the situation at hand.

"I called the reporter as soon as I learned your plane was late," she said. "He agreed to delay our meeting for a couple of hours."

"That's good to hear. I'd like to have time for a relaxing drink first." His gaze met hers. "We're on a very tight schedule."

She nodded. "Yes, I know. I understand this was the only time you had available to spend promoting your book, and your publisher wanted as much exposure as possible.''

Alex reminded himself of the stern lecture he'd received from Sam, his agent, about cooperating. "I'm afraid that's true. I didn't realize how much was involved in promoting a book."

Stephanie unconsciously took a step back, creating some needed extra space between them. She found his nearness unnerving somehow. Nodding toward the conveyor belt, which had begun to move, she said, "Why don't you claim your bags while I find someone to help us with the luggage?"

He raised one eyebrow slightly. "Why do we need help? Do you have luggage here?"

She could feel a slight flush on her cheeks. "No. I've already left my bags at the hotel. I came in on an earlier flight from New York."

"In that case I think I can manage my own bags without assistance," Alex said with a slight smile.

She watched him ease through the crowd that surrounded the luggage carousel, his wide shoulders cutting a swath through the people. He looked as though he could have managed to carry most of the luggage making the rounds. Her suggestion had been automatic for her. Stephanie was used to treating her authors like Dresden dolls. She would have to keep in mind that such an attitude toward Alexander Sloan would only alienate him.

However, there was nothing she could do about the fact that she felt in charge of the trip. It was only later, when she caught the startled look on his face, that Stephanie realized she had signaled a cabdriver at the entrance to the airport and was pointing out his bag before Alex had a chance to do so.

Once on their way, Alex settled into the seat beside her with an almost soundless sigh and gave her an amused glance. "You take your job very seriously, don't you?"

"What do you mean?"

"Were you afraid I wouldn't be able to find my way to the hotel today without you?"

Why did his polite tone set her teeth on edge? "Look, Colonel Sloan, I—"

"Alex," he corrected smoothly.

Stephanie paused, searching for her competent air of composure. "I was just going to say, Alex, that I am used to taking charge on a tour such as this. Not every writer has your sophistication. Many of them haven't traveled much and are grateful to have someone lead the way."

"So am I," he offered in a bland voice.

She looked at him, puzzled.

"Grateful," he went on by way of explanation. "Although I'm used to travel, civilian travel is considerably different. I appreciate your expertise and willingly bow to your knowledgeable leadership."

Why did she feel he was mocking her? Both his expression and his tone of voice showed nothing but cordial politeness. Only his eyes sparkled in a manner that might be interpreted as mischievous.

Stephanie forced herself not to allow his attitude to ruffle her. Returning his polite smile, she said, "You don't know how much that relieves my mind, Colonel. I appreciate your reassurance."

Turning her gaze toward the window, she refused to look at him until they reached the hotel.

Alex paid the cabdriver and retrieved his bag before she could say anything. "Since the travel expenses are being reimbursed, it will be much simpler if I pay everything, Colonel," she pointed out while he held the first door for her to enter the lobby. She didn't wait to get his reaction.

The doorman immediately grabbed the door so that Alex could follow her.

"Sorry, Stephanie," he said with a grin. "I must have forgotten myself there for a moment. I suppose my male ego couldn't handle allowing you to pay the driver. I would never be able to face the man again."

"Of course you wouldn't," she agreed sympathetically. "Who knows what sort of tales he'd spread about you around Philadelphia."

"Exactly," he said with a relieved expression that Stephanie admitted he faked very well. So the colonel had a sense of humor when it came to himself. She could forgive him many faults in exchange for not taking himself too seriously.

Stephanie stopped at the desk and asked for their keys. Without meeting his eyes she handed Alex his and said, "We have almost an hour before the interview. The reporter agreed to meet us here in the lounge at seven." She started for the elevator. "That should give us both a few moments to relax."

"Sounds good to me," he said agreeably, a little amused at her brusque tone and organized demeanor.

The elevator door opened and they both stepped in. Although Stephanie had taken the time to check in

earlier and had her bags delivered to her room, she
hadn't bothered going up herself. She wasn't worried.
Her assistant had been with her long enough to know
how to book suitable rooms. She glanced down at her
key before pushing the appropriate button for their
floor.

Getting off on the tenth floor, they walked down the
hall in silence. When Stephanie inserted the key in the
door to her room she had a sudden sinking sensation.
Alex was entering the room right next to hers.

Only then did she remember the standard instructions her assistant followed on these tours. Because she
generally traveled with women, Stephanie had gotten
into the habit of ordering connecting rooms. On a
tight schedule, she had found it simpler to have some
of their meetings in their rooms rather than always in
a public place. She hadn't given that aspect of traveling with a male author a thought. Until now.

Stephanie only had time to note that her luggage
had been placed in her room when she heard the connecting door open between their rooms.

"Hello, again," Alex drawled. Stephanie turned to
find him leaning casually against the doorjamb, his
hands stuck in his pants pockets. "It looks as though
we're going to become very well acquainted before this
trip is over."

Stephanie could feel her temper struggling to gain
the upper hand, and she fought to control it. She must
remain calm and professional, no matter what the
provocation.

"My assistant is used to my traveling with women, Colonel Sloan. Connecting rooms facilitate communications."

"They certainly do that," he agreed. "And I'm all for facilitating communications." His expression could not have been more innocent.

Taking a deep breath, Stephanie forced herself to pause a moment for control. "Colonel Sloan, you and I are going to be experiencing a very tough, oftentimes grueling ten days together. I am aware you haven't had much experience in this sort of thing, and I'm making allowances. However, there is something that we should understand right off." She watched as he slowly straightened his position in the doorway. "We are both professionals, doing our jobs. There is no reason to allow any personal feelings of any sort— whether they are filled with animosity or attraction— to get in the way. I intend to show you the respect you deserve, and I would appreciate your doing the same with me."

She stood there in the middle of the room, facing him, her chin slightly elevated.

He studied her intently for a moment, and she was suddenly reminded of the photograph of him she had in her file. Here was the man she had seen—flinty-eyed, stern-jawed, with an air of command that seemed to come naturally to him.

"I see," he said after a moment. "I wasn't aware that I was showing you anything but respect, Ms. Benson. It's true that I am unfamiliar with this type of situation. Perhaps I've been trying too hard to lighten the atmosphere somewhat, but certainly not at your expense.''

Stephanie found that she could no longer hold his steady gaze. She walked over to the windows and opened the blinds. ''We have a lovely view of the city. Have you noticed?''

When he didn't answer, she turned around. He hadn't moved from the doorway. When her gaze finally met his, he said, ''And what feelings are you experiencing at the moment, Stephanie? Animosity...or attraction?''

Colonel Sloan could be a wicked adversary, Stephanie realized with a pang. He never missed a trick. Forcing herself to meet his steady gaze once more, she said quietly, ''Neither one, Colonel Sloan. I'm just trying to do my job in the best way I know how. I haven't meant to offend you nor to flirt with you, and I apologize for getting off on the wrong foot.''

Alex continued to watch her, his gaze distinctly unnerving. ''You don't owe me an apology, Stephanie. I'm sorry that my remarks have made you uncomfortable.''

She tried to soften her response somewhat. ''I just think that while we're on the tour we shouldn't think of ourselves as members of the opposite sex. We're just two people traveling together.'' She paused, looking at him a little uncertainly.

''Makes good sense to me. I'll just think of you as one of the men, if you'd like.''

Why did she keep feeling he was making fun of her? It was due to the fact that his eyes had lost their flinty look and now seemed to have an unholy sparkle in them. Stephanie abruptly nodded. "Fine."

He stepped back and started to close the door between their rooms. "I'll see you downstairs, then—" he glanced at his wristwatch "—in about half an hour." He gave her a mock salute and a gentle smile before shutting the door.

Stephanie realized that she was trembling as she stared at the door now separating them. She had never before met a man like him. Nothing seemed to rattle or dismay him. He took everything in stride. She had always seen herself in that way, whether she was with her brothers or Kent. Stephanie could roll with the punches. She had always taken pride in being flexible and able to adjust to the situation at the moment.

Yet with Alex Sloan she felt off center. How had that happened?

Glancing at her watch, Stephanie decided she had time to have a shower before the meeting downstairs. Somehow, she had to relocate the inner serenity that helped her to keep her balance. Something told her that being around Alex Sloan would test that serenity to the utmost. For some reason that she was unable to fathom at the moment, Stephanie was rather looking forward to the testing.

She went into the shower, humming to herself.

Alex leaned back against the cushioned banquette in the dimly lit lounge of the hotel and took a sip of his drink. The room was sparsely filled, and he found the quiet background music and muffled sound of voices in conversation soothing.

He'd heard nothing from Stephanie's room when he left and had half expected to find her waiting efficiently downstairs for him to appear, but she hadn't been there when he arrived. He tried to remember their agenda for Philadelphia without resorting to the notes he had placed in his pocket. After the interview, no doubt, they'd have something to eat, then call it a night. Tomorrow there was an early-morning television interview, a luncheon where he was to speak and a phone-in radio talk show at four o'clock. Then they were to catch an evening flight to Denver.

Would all of this help to sell his books, he wondered? Did it make any difference to a reader whether an author were personable, had the ability to stand before a group of people and talk without being tongue-tied and could field unrehearsed questions with aplomb? Or was a reader more interested in a good plot and vivid characterizations?

At this point in his career, Alex had no idea and could only bow to the superior experience and knowledge of his agent and publisher.

He thought back over his career and all that he had experienced that had gone into the shaping of his abilities. He'd been forced to deal with the press more than he cared to because of the number of hot spots where he'd been stationed over the years. He hoped discussing his book wouldn't be quite the same. He was not dealing with classified information now; only his imagination.

Glancing toward the door, his imagination suddenly flared into a series of unexpected fantasies. Stephanie Benson stood outlined in the doorway, the soft, flowing dress she wore emphasizing the long expanse of well-shaped legs. She had pulled her hair into a topknot at the crown of her head, and soft wispy curls fell across her forehead and in front of her ears.

She looked as though she could be meeting a lover, and Alex felt a sudden jolt at the thought. What was it about this woman that made him so aware of her? He'd been around women more beautiful, but none that made him feel as though his whole body was a quivering antenna whenever she walked into a room.

Alex stood up and watched as she spotted him and smiled. The smile caught him off guard. It came unexpectedly, naturally, as though they were old friends or, perhaps, the lovers he'd first imagined when he saw her standing there.

With a natural grace, she approached him through the cluster of empty tables and chairs, silently accepting his gesture to sit down beside him.

"You're very prompt, Colonel," she said, her voice a little breathless.

"It's amazing what the lure of a good drink will do for a person," he replied, sitting down beside her. Alex signaled the waitress and waited while Stephanie ordered and received a glass of wine. Picking up his glass, he touched it lightly to hers. "Here's to a successful tour," he said with a smile.

Stephanie was having trouble catching her breath. She felt as though she'd been racing since she'd gotten out of the shower. She refused to consider the reason why she'd been so eager to get downstairs. All of this was part of her job.

"Do you know the reporter who's supposed to meet us?" he asked, placing his arm along the back of the banquette behind her shoulders.

She shook her head, suddenly aware of how close they were. "No. He was going to check the desk first before coming in here. So far no one has done that." She attempted to move away from him slightly. "I suppose now we sit and try to spot him when he comes in. At least the desk will tell him we're already here."

Stephanie could hear herself rattling on, desperately trying to sound nonchalant and at ease while they waited. She tried to ignore the delicious scent of Alex's after-shave and wished the banquette was a little larger. His thigh rested firmly against hers. Her body seemed to be registering his presence over its entire surface.

"What do you bet that's him," Alex said after a few moments of silence, nodding toward the door.

Stephanie glanced up with a feeling of relief. A young man carrying a camera case came striding through the doorway and looked around. Once again Alex stood up. The man hastened over and stuck out his hand.

"Hi! I'm Mike Malone. Sorry to keep you waiting. I wasn't sure how much time you'd need, with your plane running late."

"There's no problem," Alex said with a smile. "It was nice to have a few moments to relax." He motioned to Stephanie. "This is Stephanie Benson."

Mike's eyes widened slightly and took on an appreciative gleam. He sat down in the chair across from them and nodded to Stephanie. "It's good to meet you after our phone conversations." He pulled out a pad and pen and explained in an apologetic tone, ''I'm working on a tight deadline, so if you don't mind, we'll get started.''

Stephanie sat back and listened quietly. The reporter knew his job and had done his homework. He'd obviously read *Bridges to Burn* and had several pertinent questions and comments to make.

She remembered her reaction to the book when she had first read it. She'd been surprised at the depth and strength shown in a first novel. Kent had predicted that Alex would go to the top of the list of bestselling writers once people discovered him.

He'd obviously done his research. Stephanie had been so caught up in the story that she had almost felt abandoned when the book ended. Alex Sloan certainly knew how to keep a reader's interest. The sustained suspense had kept her turning the pages until well past midnight.

The reporter was pointing out similar reactions on his part.

Stephanie watched Alex surreptitiously from the corner of her eye and noted how diplomatically he handled the reporter's questions. Obviously, he was no novice, neatly sidestepping questions he didn't want to answer and moving the subject away from sensitive issues.

She needn't have concerned herself that this man would require any help from her in this area. No doubt he was just as good at giving speeches. At least she hoped so, since he was scheduled for at least one in each of the cities they were visiting.

Eventually, Mike and Alex paused in their conversation while Mike quickly reviewed his notes. He glanced up with a grin. "Well, Colonel Sloan, I believe you've answered all my questions and given me a great deal to think about." He stood up and stuck out his hand. "Good luck, sir, with the sale of your book. I predict it's going to be quite popular. Maybe we'll see it as a movie one of these days."

Alex also stood and shook the younger man's hand. "I suppose that's a possibility, but I'm certainly not anticipating anything in that regard at the moment."

Mike shook Stephanie's hand, waved to them both, and strode out of the room.

Alex picked up the new glass that the waitress had recently placed in front of him and took a sip, then looked at Stephanie. "How did I do?"

As though he had the least doubt. Stephanie smiled. "You did just fine, Colonel Sloan, sir," she said in a lazy tone, "just fine."

Alex stretched. He slightly loosened his tie. "Does that mean I'm off duty now and we can go eat? I'm starved."

The "little boy" appeal certainly wasn't wasted on her. Once again his arm was behind her, so that he effectively blocked her from moving. "By all means, Colonel. We don't want you wasting away to nothing, you know."

He stood up and assisted her to her feet. The solid strength that he radiated gave no indication of lack of nourishment. Stephanie led the way from the lounge, idly noting how crowded it had become while they were there. She also noted that every female in the place seemed to become aware of the man following behind her.

Admit it, he'd turn feminine heads wherever he was. If he found it difficult to make a living as a writer, she could think of several other occupations where he'd be a natural.

"I thought we might eat here at the hotel, if that's all right with you," she said, pausing in the lobby to look at him.

"Suits me." They followed the directions to one of the restaurants located on the top floor and were seated at a table for two near a wide picture window.

"Nice place," Alex commented.

"Yes. The publisher wanted you to be as comfortable as possible."

Alex looked up from the menu. "I'll have to admit that many of the places I've spent time in couldn't begin to compare with all of this." He nodded to the ornately decorated room.

Stephanie studied the man across from her for a moment. After the waiter left with their order, she said, "I have read your biography so often I feel as though I could recite it by memory, but there is so much that it doesn't say."

He leaned forward slightly, resting his arms on the table. "Such as?"

"Where you've spent those twenty-two years of military service, what you were doing, what made you decide to write a book."

"Now you're sounding like that reporter."

"Am I? I noticed that when he asked similar questions, you managed to subtly change the subject."

He grinned. "You noticed that, did you? I can't put anything past you, can I?"

"Just as you're changing the subject now. Why don't you want to talk about your background?"

"Mostly because it's repetitious and boring. I moved around a lot, but I did the same types of things. Some places were worse than others. I stayed at some places longer than others. Over all, it evened itself out." He leaned back in his chair. "I don't have anything to complain about."

"Did you request your latest assignment?"

His eyes narrowed slightly. He toyed with the silver by his plate for a moment, then replied, "Let's say it was a mutual agreement."

"Do you like what you're doing now?"

"It's necessary."

"Do you miss being overseas?"

"At times."

"Is that why you decided to write your book?"

"Partly. I suppose I felt that I had something to say, something that other people might want to read."

"I'm impressed with your book."

He smiled. "Aren't you paid to be?"

"No. And generally I keep my opinions to myself. I noticed that you were willing to discuss the book, but not your reasons for choosing that particular topic."

He shrugged. "I'm interested in the Asian culture. I've spent many years in the area. I wanted to try my hand at creating a window for others to view what might happen to that part of the world."

"If it hasn't already," she said softly.

Their meal arrived and Stephanie noticed that Alex seemed to be relieved with the interruption.

The more she became acquainted with Colonel Alex Sloan, the more intriguing Stephanie found him. She wondered if he would allow her to get to know him better in the coming days and why that should matter to her. It wasn't necessary that she befriend the man. He was a client...a product to sell. Stephanie wasn't sure just what it was about him that she found so fascinating...and so dangerous to her peace of mind.

He was different from any of the men she had known. Her father and brothers had all been very open and easygoing. There had been nothing mysterious or elusive about them. She had gravitated to a similar personality when she met Kent. Perhaps that was why they had become so comfortable so quickly.

Up until now, if anyone had told her that what she felt for Kent was more brotherly than loverlike, she would have vehemently denied the statement. However, now that she had met Alex Sloan, Stephanie realized that he was creating feelings within her that she had never before experienced.

For the first time since Kent had told her about his reaction to Susan, she felt as though she could identify the feelings he had tried to explain. No wonder he had felt confused. There was no rational explanation for what seemed to be happening to her.

Although she had no intention of following through her reactions to Alex, Stephanie knew without a doubt that if she were still engaged to Kent, she would be upset that another man could create such a confusion of feelings within her.

Was this what Kent had faced? Could she have been as honest with him under similar circumstances?

For the first time in two weeks, Stephanie could think about Kent without experiencing a painful ache in her chest.

Three

—

Stephanie forced herself to relax when the Fasten Seat Belts/No Smoking sign flashed off in the airplane cabin. No matter how often she flew, she knew that she'd never get used to it. There seemed to be something so unnatural about hurtling through the air at such a ridiculous speed. The long climb to their designated altitude had seemed to take forever, but now they had leveled off.

"You surprise me, Stephanie," Alex said in a low voice near her right ear. "I wouldn't have expected you to be afraid to fly."

She turned her head to stare at him and said, "I'm not afraid. Whatever gave you that idea?"

He grinned. "I'm not sure. It could have been the lack of color in your face." He glanced down at the armrest between them. "Or it could have been the way your fingernails have been digging into the back of my hand."

Horrified, she, too looked down and saw that, instead of gripping the armrest as she had done with her left hand, she had made several small crescent-shaped dents in the back of his hand. Embarrassed, she jerked her hand away. "I'm really very sorry. I don't know why I didn't realize—I mean, you should have said—"

"No permanent damage done. I would have thought that you were used to flying, that's all."

Wearily, she leaned her head back against the seat and closed her eyes. "I can't imagine ever getting used to it. I just manage to tolerate it, that's all."

His quiet chuckle seemed to soothe rather than ridicule. She smiled and opened her eyes. "Did I really go white?"

He nodded. "You really did." He studied each of her features carefully. "However, you seem to be all right now."

No doubt. With his gaze wandering over her face, she could feel the warmth of color flood her cheeks.

Stephanie was glad when the flight attendant paused to see if they wanted pillows or magazines, drawing Alex's attention away from her. She glanced out the window, although there was nothing to see. It had been dark when they left Philadelphia. They would be going through two time zones before reaching Denver, but even so, it would be after ten o'clock local time before they arrived there.

The day had gone well. Thank God they had made all their connections smoothly. There had been a good

turnout for Alex's speech, and he had handled the
questions at the end with skill and diplomacy. She had
been impressed.

Actually, there was a great deal concerning Alex
about which to be impressed. Didn't the man have any
weaknesses? He appeared to be as fresh and relaxed
now, fourteen hours after their day had begun, as he
had in the beginning. He had charmed the host on the
early-morning television show with his humor and
low-key discussion and had carried that relaxed attitude into the radio show.

Stephanie wished she didn't have the niggling little
feeling that they were experiencing the lull before the
storm. Of course, she didn't expect the tour to be
without unexpected problems—none of them were.
She and Alex were very fortunate that their first stop
had gone so smoothly.

She closed her eyes. Stephanie had learned early to
use any time available to rest and recuperate. Tomorrow was going to be another hectic day. However, she
felt much better about the tour now that she had seen
Alex in action. He was going to do just fine.

When they arrived at the hotel several hours later,
Stephanie was handed a fistful of messages. She almost groaned. What could be wrong now? Quickly
shuffling through them, she relaxed somewhat. Three
were from coordinators of the local publicity, letting
her know that they would be in touch with her the next
morning. That wasn't so bad. Two were personal—
Laura had called, and so had her brother, Dave.

Dave lived near Santa Fe, New Mexico. They rarely
got to see each other but were so in tune that when-

ever they had a chance to talk, they picked up where they had previously left off without missing a beat. His message was typical.

"If you'd stay in one place more than a few hours, I'd come see you. Give me a call and I'll try to come up."

When she'd called him the week before, he'd been out, so she left a message with his housekeeper that she would be in Denver, telling him the hotel where she would be staying. Obviously, he was following up.

"Must be good news, from the expression on your face," Alex remarked idly as they rode the elevator to their floor.

She smiled. "Yes, it is. One of my brothers is going to try to meet me here." She looked back down at the pink slip in her hand. "I don't want to get too excited, in case he can't manage to get away."

"Where does he live?"

"Santa Fe."

"Is that your home?"

The elevator doors opened and she stepped out ahead of him. "Oh, no. I was born near Sacramento and have family scattered all over the country. I consider New York my home now."

At least this time she didn't have to explain about their rooms. Once again there were connecting doors. He opened the door and walked through, checking her room.

"Is something wrong?" she asked, puzzled by his manner.

He shook his head. "Just wanted to be sure everything was secure."

She almost laughed. Did he really see her as the little woman who needed protection? Shaking her head slightly, she walked over and opened her suitcase. He paused at the door between the rooms. "I think I'll order something to drink. Would you like anything?"

Stephanie glanced at her watch. It was already past midnight, mountain time, but she also realized she was a little keyed up. Maybe a glass of wine would help her to relax.

She agreed and told him what she wanted. When he closed the door behind him, she began to hang up the clothes she intended to wear the next day. Was it too late to return Laura's call tonight? Of course it was, but she knew she wouldn't be able to go to sleep until she knew what Laura had wanted.

Deciding to place the call before showering, Stephanie quickly undressed and slipped on her peach housecoat, then sat down on the bed and dialed the apartment number.

The phone rang several times before she heard a muffled voice.

"Hi, Laura. I just got into my hotel. Sorry to wake you up."

"Oh, that's okay. I tried to stay awake, but must have drifted off."

"So what's up?"

"You'll probably think I'm being silly, but I was concerned about how you were doing. So I called your hotel in Philadelphia, but you had already checked out. Then I decided to leave word at your next destination. Are you holding up okay?"

Stephanie smiled. Finding Laura playing mother hen was an interesting switch.

"I'm fine, Laura."

"You're sure? I know you're convinced that you and Wonder Woman are sisters, but you'd tell me if it's too much for you, wouldn't you?"

"Of course I would. You know me better than to think I'd lie about it."

"So is the colonel giving you a hard time? I mean, do you have to salute every time you see him, and pace along two steps behind him everywhere you go?"

Stephanie laughed. "He's nothing like that, you screwball. He seems to be—" She heard a tap on the connecting door. "Just a moment, Laura." Raising her voice, slightly, she said, "Come on in."

Hearing her invitation, Alex opened the door, then picked up their glasses and walked through to Stephanie's room. When he caught a glimpse of her, he felt as though he'd suddenly been hit in the solar plexus with a fist. She'd turned off the overhead light so that the lamp by the bed made a halo of brightness where she sat. She'd changed clothes. He'd never seen her as anything but businesslike. Until now. The thin, satin material lovingly molded the curves of her figure, and the light from the lamp picked up the highlights of her hair.

She smiled when she saw him. "Thank you," she mouthed silently and held out her hand while holding the phone at her ear. Stephanie nodded toward a chair in the corner, silently inviting him to stay.

Alex handed her the glass, unable to take his eyes off of her. Without giving his actions much thought, he followed her instructions and sank into the chair, unabashedly listening to her conversation.

"That was Alex," she explained into the phone so that Laura would know why she could no longer continue their topic of conversation. "He brought me a glass of wine to help me unwind."

"Oho!" Laura chortled. "So you decided to take my advice after all!" Stephanie had just lifted the glass in a slight toast to Alex and placed the wine to her lips when Laura made her remark.

Alex watched with interest as Stephanie suddenly jerked the glass from her lips, almost spilling the liquid. He enjoyed watching the rosy hue that seemed to engulf her face and wondered what had just been said to create such an abrupt reaction.

She tried to laugh. "Don't be silly, Laura. The tour is going quite well." Before Laura could say anything further, Stephanie hurried into speech once more. "I know it's late for you so I'll let you go. I'll call in a few days with an update, okay?" she said, refusing to look at Alex.

"Make sure you're alone when you call, sweetie. I want to hear all the details."

"Good night, Laura," Stephanie said firmly and hung up the phone.

Alex spoke as soon as she put the phone down. "I'm sorry if it embarrassed you for me to stay, Stephanie. I guess I wasn't thinking."

She waved her hand, then picked up the glass she had recently abandoned and swallowed some of the wine. "It wasn't your fault. I have a roommate with a weird sense of humor."

"She must have wondered what I was doing in your room at this time of night," he offered with a smile.

"How did you—?" She stopped, realizing that she had just confirmed his suspicions. "She just likes to tease. I don't pay much attention to her."

"I think it shows a rather caring relationship myself. After all, here you are, traveling with a stranger..."

"You aren't exactly a stranger, you know."

"Perhaps. But you have no idea what I might be like when there's just the two of us."

She gave him a level gaze. "I'm not worried about it."

He met her gaze with an equally level stare. "Maybe you should be," he said softly. No matter how quietly he had spoken, the challenge was there.

Stephanie supposed it was only natural that sooner or later he would test the waters, so to speak. After all, they were going to be spending an inordinate amount of time together. Perhaps he was used to casual relationships, affairs that meant nothing more than a few hours of mutual pleasure. Unbidden, the question came: how did she know there would be pleasure?

Who was she kidding? Alexander Sloan was the type of man who was sensitive to other people. That sensitivity was what made his book so striking. He would never take his pleasure without giving equal amounts in return.

What was she thinking about, anyway? She didn't care how sensitive he was, she was not interested in getting involved with him.

What confused her at the moment was why she had invited him to stay and share their drinks. It wasn't surprising that he might presume from her invitation that she was willing to share something more. What was it about Alex that made her react so out of character toward him?

When Stephanie focused on Alex's expression once more, she found him smiling while he sat there in the chair, looking more relaxed than she had ever seen him. When her gaze met his, he said, "I wish I'd had a camera to record the myriad expressions that have crossed your face in the last few moments."

She'd forgotten that one of his skills was the ability to read people. Stephanie tried to shrug it off. "I was thinking about Laura," she lied. "And how fortunate I was to make such a friend."

"What does she do?"

"She's an editor for a fashion magazine. I met her through Harry Mattingly, whom I work for. I was fresh from the West Coast and she took me under her wing and taught me how to get around in Manhattan."

Alex nodded, allowing her to sidestep his earlier comment. He recognized her ploy for what it was. She had successfully defused what could have been a sexually provocative moment for them. Okay. So she had let him know in the most subtle way possible that she wasn't interested in him. That was fine, except for one minor problem. Alex discovered that he was sure as hell interested in her.

What was he thinking of, anyway? This was a business trip, after all. Why create a situation that would make their working together fraught with tension? But wasn't the tension going to be there, anyway, whether or not they actually made love?

He was too aware of her not to recognize that she was equally aware of him. He could almost see the vibrations that bounced between them the moment they were in the same room together.

So what was he going to do about it? Obviously, she was choosing to ignore it. He glanced down at the half-empty glass. Maybe this wasn't such a good idea, after all. The more he relaxed, the more innovative some of his thoughts became.

Alex yawned and leaned forward in the chair. "Guess I'd better go to bed before I fall asleep right here. You might find that a little hard to explain."

"You're right," she agreed lightly, standing up. "I didn't thank you earlier for the drink. It was very kind of you to offer."

Alex drained his glass and set it on the table beside his chair. "Glad to be of service, ma'am," he drawled.

She felt the tension between them but didn't know what to do about it. What was it about the man, anyway? He made no overt moves. He'd accepted her lack of response to him with charming nonchalance, and at the moment seemed no more threatening than a house cat. So why did she keep visualizing a jungle cat being mistakenly invited into the house?

Walking over to the door to his room, she turned around, only to find him right behind her. "Uh, well, I guess I'll see you in the morning, then. We could meet for breakfast if you'd like."

"I'd like that very much." He stood beside her, looking down, and it was almost as if she could feel his body heat touching her, yet he was almost a foot away.

Forcing herself to gaze up at him, she said calmly, "Good night."

She looked like the most proper young lady imaginable, standing there, seeing an unwanted suitor to the door. Alex couldn't remember when he'd enjoyed a woman's personality so much. He felt a sudden impulse to grab her and whirl her around in a breathless circle, just to celebrate the fact that he now knew such a woman existed.

Stephanie was such a mixture of opposing characteristics—brusque, yet at times shy; professional, yet at times a little unsure of herself; intelligent, yet with a charming touch of naiveté.

Despite the attraction he felt for her, Alex knew that for the next week or so he was going to have to school himself to hide his growing feelings from her. *Just remember to keep it light,* he reminded himself.

Stephanie found herself holding her breath as he walked past her into his room. Releasing the air in her lungs, she sighed softly, only to discover she had relaxed too soon. Alex turned and placed his finger under her chin. Lifting it slightly, he said, "Pleasant dreams," and placed his lips on hers.

Had he tried to embrace her in any way, Stephanie would have immediately sprung away from him. But he didn't. The light pressure of his finger under her chin was a very soft caress. And his lips—ah, his lips. How could she possibly resist the tenderness of his mouth softly pressed against hers?

He didn't try to create additional intimacy between them. However, he was in no hurry to break away, either. His mouth felt firm against hers, yet there was no bruising pressure. She had no feeling that he was preparing to pounce. He gently explored her mouth, his tongue lightly flicking against her lips until she unconsciously opened them. Still without touching her anywhere else, he continued to gently mold and re-shape her mouth until it willingly clung to his, reluctant for him to release her.

The kiss was a statement that stood alone—a touching, a sharing, a willingness to communicate on a fundamental—a nonverbal level.

Stephanie was understandably captivated. When Alex eventually stepped away from her, she had trouble for a moment forcing her eyes to open. When she did, the look she found in his eyes made her quiver. There was no denying the desire she saw there, yet the desire was at odds with the tenderness and lack of aggression he had demonstrated.

Alex obviously had control over himself. Stephanie sensed that in no way was he going to act upon the emotions he was feeling at the moment. She almost resented his self-control. Not that she wanted him to continue the kiss, but she found that she was having difficulty with her own response to him.

Jerkily, she turned away from him and waited for him to close the door. The solid noise of wood against wood seemed to release her from the sense of paraly-sis she was feeling.

What is happening to me? she wondered, automat-ically walking into the bathroom and turning on the shower. Shedding her housecoat, she stepped under the spray and absently began to soap herself. *He kissed me.* So what? A lot of people had kissed her. Her family, her friends, Kent.

Kent. She was behaving the same way he had about Susan. Over a kiss. She had wondered at the time if he had told her the whole truth. Could one kiss cause such a reaction that a person would suddenly question his or her feelings about another relationship?

Without a doubt.

What was so different about Alex's kiss?

There had been nothing in the kiss that would have been out of place or inappropriate, even if they had been in the lobby of the hotel. It was a gentle goodnight kiss. And yet her body still seemed to be tingling from the brief contact.

Determined not to give the kiss one more thought, Stephanie could think of nothing else as she prepared for bed. After brushing her teeth, she glanced in the mirror and wondered at the half-dazed expression she wore. It was only a kiss, for crying out loud. One little, very ordinary kiss.

As she tossed and turned during the night, she wondered why her glass of wine hadn't helped her to unwind after such a hectic day.

Perhaps it was the brand.

By the time Stephanie finally fell into a deep sleep she was exhausted, and the next morning she almost overslept. Her travel alarm had been ringing steadily before she came awake enough to reach for it.

Feeling as though she'd been out all night, she forced herself to sit up and take notice of the new day.

She would love to blame her condition on jet lag. Unfortunately, she was moving cross-country in the wrong direction for that. It was two hours later in New York than her watch was presently recording. She would have been to work hours ago if she was at home.

Of course, yesterday had been hectic. And today was going to be equally full. Forcing herself to stand, she wandered into the bathroom and looked at her bleary eyes and puffy lids. Stephanie decided to try a shower, hoping it would wake her up.

The shower probably helped, but what really opened her eyes to their widest was a tap on the bathroom door and a deep voice that said, "Telephone, Stephanie."

It had only taken two words from that particular man to accomplish what the past fifteen minutes had been unable to do. Hastily turning off the water, she grabbed a towel and briskly dried herself. Then she jerked on her robe and opened the bathroom door.

The connecting door between their rooms was open, and she could see Alex standing in front of the mirror in his bathroom, shaving, wearing only a pair of slacks. He seemed unconcerned with his half-dressed appearance and Stephanie attempted to take his unclothed condition in stride. However, she found herself staring at his broad chest that was so faithfully reproduced in the mirror.

"When the phone rang, I figured you couldn't hear it over the sound of the water, so I answered it for you," he explained with a smile, then went back to shaving.

She nodded, suddenly remembering the reason she had come out of the bathroom. Hurrying toward the phone, she picked it up. "Hello?"

"Who the hell was that?" Dave demanded to know in his most irate, brotherly voice. "Kent isn't traveling with you, is he?"

Oh, dear Lord. Just what she needed to start off her day. In as cheerful a tone as she could manage, Stephanie said, "Oh, Dave, it's so good to hear from you. Are you really going to be able to fly to Denver today?" Surely he would get the message and realize this wasn't the time to discuss her telephone answering devices.

Obviously, that was too much to hope for. "Since when have you taken up sharing your room, Sis?"

"Sorry I didn't return your call yesterday," she continued doggedly, "but by the time we checked in, I knew you'd be asleep."

"We? Who we?"

"I told your housekeeper to tell you that I'm touring with Colonel Sloan to promote his book."

"Yes, she told me. However, I didn't realize the publisher was economizing to such an extent that you were forced to share your room."

"Dave, please stop talking like an irate father. It's a little too early in the morning for me to deal with you."

"Is that supposed to make me feel any better? If so, I'm not at all reassured."

Why did life have to become complicated so early in the morning? "I'm sorry, Dave. I guess I'm just not making myself very clear. I didn't get much sleep last night."

Oh, no. That made it even worse. "What I mean is, we're keeping a tight schedule. Alex heard the phone ringing from his room. Since we have connecting rooms and he heard my shower going, he was considerate enough to answer it for me."

There was a pause before Dave responded. "I was planning to fly up today, anyway. Now I know I'm coming to see you. What does Kent think about your traveling with Colonel Sloan and this business of connecting doors?"

"Uh, well, we need to talk about that, too, Dave. It's been a while, hasn't it?"

"More than I realized."

"When can you be here?" she asked, thinking about the upcoming interrogation she was going to be subjected to and wondering why anyone would want to have brothers.

"How about five o'clock?"

"That will be fine. I'll see you then."

"And I want to meet your colonel."

"He isn't my colonel, Dave. Besides, he may very well want some free time of his own this evening. I thought that you and I could have dinner together and catch up on all the family news."

"I certainly intend to do that. And I also intend to meet Colonel Sloan."

Stephanie sighed once again. "Yes, Dave." She knew better than to argue. And to think that she found his persistence an endearing quality when he was growing up. Just shows how a person's perspective can change.

She hung up the phone with a certain amount of relief, knowing that she was only postponing the inquisition. All right, so maybe she should have requested different rooms once she realized how they would be traveling. Dave would immediately spot the weak logic when she explained that she hadn't thought about it.

She hadn't.

What did it matter anyway? She wasn't a teenager, for Pete's sake. She'd been on her own for years.

Maybe he'd only been teasing her. She wished.

Stephanie was thankful to discover that Alex had shut the door between their rooms, giving her conversation some privacy. She returned to the bathroom and began to prepare her face and hair. She would have to tell Alex of Dave's upcoming visit. Surely Alex would like some time for himself. She didn't think she could bear to explain about Kent in Alex's presence.

Dave had never met Kent, but her brother had seemed pleased about their engagement when she talked to him at Christmas. She knew she would have to tell him about the broken engagement. She also knew that she would find the task easier to do face-to-face. What she hadn't considered was the possibility of Alex Sloan being so helpful as to answer her blasted phone.

Glancing back at her image in the mirror, she realized that she'd certainly come awake since the phone call. She wasn't sure who she had to thank for that.

Stephanie had never before realized how much more comfortable it had been to tour with chattering romance writers. She vowed never to complain about them again.

Four

—

I'm sorry if I caused you any problems this morning by answering your phone,'' Alex said after they had completed their breakfast.

Stephanie gratefully clutched her cup with both hands, basking in the warmth while she sipped her coffee. She carefully set the cup down before looking at him. ''There was no problem, really. It was my brother, Dave.''

''I realized when I heard his voice that I have never asked if you were married or engaged. I seem to have spent most of the time we've been together apologizing to you. I have no excuse for my behavior last night, but I want you to know that I'm aware I was way out of line.'' His eyes crinkled at the corners as though he were smiling. ''Hardly the behavior of an officer and a gentleman,'' he added.

His gaze made her feel as though she were pinned beneath a piercing beam of light. She could feel her cheeks glowing and knew that he would see the flush his remarks had created.

Stephanie wished she knew what it was about this man that reduced her to a stammering, blushing idiot. All he had done was kiss her. There had been no groping or pawing. He had no cause to apologize.

"You don't owe me any apologies, Alex, for either last night or this morning. Let's just forget it, okay?"

"Whatever you say, ma'am."

His formal military response stopped her for a moment. Then she forced herself to go on. "My brother is going to be here this evening. I'd like you to meet him if possible. However, you would probably find an evening spent listening to us discuss family happenings rather boring. So if you'd like to do something on your own..."

"Sounds good. I have several friends living here in Denver. I'll see if any of them are available for the evening."

Stephanie realized she'd been holding her breath. She should have known he didn't need a baby-sitter while on tour. "Fine." Pushing back her chair, she said, "We'd better head over to the television studio, don't you think?"

Alex noticed her obvious relief and wondered about it. Was she so uncomfortable around him that she was pleased at the thought that she didn't have to spend the evening with him?

He stood up and placed his hand in the small of her back, escorting her from the hotel restaurant.

* * *

Their arrival at the television studio seemed almost anticlimactic. Teresa Sinclair, the woman who would be interviewing Alex on the air, greeted them warmly. After showing Stephanie where she could sit to watch the interview, Teresa led Alex to what appeared to be the cozy corner of someone's living room. As soon as they were seated, a young man came over and fastened a small microphone to the lapel of Alex's suit, while Teresa quickly fastened a similar device beneath a ruffle of her feminine blouse.

Given a little distance from him, Stephanie was able to study the man with whom she had been thrown into rather intimate circumstances. His hair shone under the bright lights, and his eyes were a startling contrast to his tanned skin. Stephanie noted that Teresa seemed to be enjoying their pre-show chat very much. Alex said something that caused Teresa to laugh, and his own grin flashed. He certainly showed no nervousness.

Stephanie almost envied him his ability to relax. Although she could instruct others on how to conduct themselves before an audience with no problem, as soon as the microphones and cameras were turned on her, she froze and her brain turned into a form of yogurt, without a hint of a thought or an intelligent spark.

While she sat there musing, the program began. She brought her attention back to the two people beneath the lights in time to hear Teresa say, "It is certainly a pleasure to have you in our studios today, Colonel Sloan. If those watching have not yet had an opportunity to read *Bridges to Burn*, I would like to recommend it.'' She reached over and picked up one of the books that Stephanie had given her earlier. ''What made you decide to write a novel?'' she asked with a smile. ''Have you always wanted to write?''

Alex ignored the camera and looked at her. ''No, I haven't, although I'm an avid reader. I suppose the story that appears in my book kept popping into my head so often that I finally wrote it down in the hopes of getting rid of it.''

''Would you say that it's autobiographical?''

''No.''

''However, your protagonist is in the air force.''

''Yes.''

''I noticed you dedicated your book to a friend named Steve. Was he, perhaps, instrumental in getting you to write?''

''Not really. Steve and I met at the Air Force Academy, years ago. We've been friends ever since.''

''You have some interesting views on what could happen to Asia in the coming years. Is that something that you've gleaned from your military experience?''

Alex smiled. ''Not at all. It was gleaned entirely from my imagination.''

''I understand that you are currently assigned to the Pentagon.''

''That's correct.''

''Could you tell us a few details about what you do there?''

His smile widened. ''I could, but I would have your audience dozing off very shortly.''

Teresa answered his smile. "I'm sure none of us would find anything you said to be boring."

My God, Stephanie thought. Why doesn't she just proposition him on the air and be done with it? The looks Teresa had been giving him were sizzling enough to start a brushfire.

Stephanie didn't have to be concerned with Alex's ability to give impressive nonanswers to any question he didn't want to respond to and to make the interviewer like it.

She wondered what his duties were at the Pentagon and how long he would be there. When she realized where her thoughts had drifted, she forced herself to pay attention to what was going on before the cameras.

"Well, Alex, I am certain all of our viewers will want to get a chance to meet you in person." She turned toward the camera with a very professional smile. "Alexander Sloan will be at Derringer's department store from one o'clock until three this afternoon, in the book section, for those of you who would like an autographed copy of *Bridges to Burn.*"

She glanced at a technician who was giving her a signal. "Thank you for being with us today, Colonel Sloan. We've enjoyed having you." Turning back to the camera, Teresa continued, "Meanwhile, stay tuned for clips of one of Hollywood's finest actors in his latest role, right after this."

As soon as the lights of the camera went off, Teresa turned to Alex and placed her hand on his lapel, ostensibly to remove the microphone. Stephanie noticed that they were in low-voiced conversation until

Teresa once again received a signal and she reluctantly bid Alex goodbye.

Stephanie waited until they were out of the station before she said, "You appeared to handle the interview well."

"Thank you."

"Have you had training in this sort of thing?"

"Not really, no."

"But this tour isn't your first time on television."

He laughed. "No."

She stopped and looked at him. "Is there any reason why you have to be so mysterious?"

"Mysterious? Me?" he asked with astonishment. "I don't know what you're talking about."

"I'm talking about how you learned to deal with the press, with the public, so well."

"Oh. I've been overseas at different times and have been asked to report on some of the situations there, that's all."

That's all? Anything newsworthy enough to have overseas correspondents asking questions of military personnel would have to be potentially explosive. Somehow, Alex made it sound like a rather dull tea party.

Yet there had been a singular lack of dull tea parties in his book. What he had written about in lucid, gripping detail let the reader know that he had personally witnessed what he so graphically described.

And he refused to discuss it.

By the time they returned to the hotel it was almost five o'clock, and Stephanie, for one, was glad to call it a day. Alex seemed to have gotten his second wind. She wondered how he did it.

They walked into the lobby, and a tall, tawny-haired man got up from a chair near a potted palm and started toward them. His western-cut suit and boots set off his rangy length and lean build.

"Dave!"

Stephanie launched herself into her brother's arms. He paused long enough to give her a hug, then looked at Alex. "I'm Dave Benson. You must be Colonel Sloan." He held out his hand as he met Alex's steady gaze.

"I'm pleased to meet you, Dave," Alex responded with a smile. "Call me Alex."

"Are you going to join us for dinner?" Dave asked.

Alex immediately shook his head. "No. I've made other plans, but thank you, anyway."

"You must have time for a drink with us," Dave insisted, and Stephanie almost groaned out loud. Surely he wasn't going to embarrass her in front of her client. He wouldn't. Stephanie just wished she had more faith in that statement.

If only she could excuse herself and go to her room for a half hour of peace and solitude. Stephanie felt as though she had been running all day. Forcing herself to relax, she smiled at both men and said, "I don't know about you, but a drink would go very well with me."

Alex returned her smile, encouraged enough by her attitude to accept Dave's invitation. They walked into the lounge together and sat down. Stephanie made sure they found a large enough table that she didn't have to share close quarters with anyone.

No sooner had they given their order than Dave said, "I was impressed with your book, Alex. You're quite a writer."

Alex smiled. "Thank you." He could sense the younger man's curiosity, as well as a hint of hostility, and he fought down his amusement. Obviously, Dave considered protecting his sister a family obligation.

"What do you think of the tour so far?" Dave asked.

"That's a little hard for me to decide. I've never done anything like this before." He glanced at Stephanie. "Your sister would be better able to tell you."

Stephanie spoke up. "Actually, everything has been going very smoothly so far. I'm amazed, but very thankful." She smiled at Alex. "Colonel Sloan is a natural in front of a crowd. He really knows how to handle people well."

Dave looked at both of them. "Have you known each other long?"

Stephanie bit her lower lip to keep from yelling at him.

"We just met two days ago," Alex said calmly.

"You seem to have gotten rather well acquainted for such a short time."

"Dave," Stephanie said in a firm voice. "We are working together on a very tight schedule. I get to know all the authors I work with quickly and well. There's nothing at all unusual about that."

"Do you travel with male authors much?"

This time both men waited for her answer with interest.

"No, as a matter of fact, I haven't. I suppose Harry thought I was probably adult enough to handle it, though. Too bad my younger—" she stressed the word "—brother doesn't seem to think so."

She was gratified to see the flush on Dave's face. The curse of blond people was their thin skin that couldn't hide the embarrassing color that sometimes betrayed them.

"I didn't mean that— You misunderstood. I was only—"

"I know exactly what you meant, Dave. I'm almost thirty years old now." Alex glanced at her in surprise. He'd thought she was at least five years younger. "I haven't needed a chaperon in a good many years."

Alex decided it was time to do some pacifying. "I understand how you feel, Dave. If I had a sister, I would probably be reacting in the same way. This whole thing is my fault, you know. I heard Stephanie's phone ringing this morning and knew she couldn't hear it. I thought it might be a call she didn't want to miss, so I dashed next door and answered it. I've already apologized to her, and now I offer my sincere apologies to you."

The two men studied each other in silence, a masculine recognition that left Stephanie totally out. The look bespoke of challenge, of acceptance and of mutual understanding. When Dave smiled, Stephanie let out the breath she was unconsciously holding.

Their drinks arrived, and Dave toasted them and the success of their tour. For the next half hour they indulged in pleasant, nonthreatening conversation.

It was only later, while she was having dinner with Dave, that she realized how successfully Alex had handled the potential confrontation. Of course, he was older and had considerably more experience in dealing with people.

"I like your colonel, Sis," Dave said, interrupting her introspection. And that, perhaps, summed up Alex's skill. He had handled Dave well, and made him like it.

She shook her head with exasperation. "I wish you would get it out of your head that Colonel Sloan and I are on some kind of long-term date, Dave. This is business. I travel with authors for a living. The fact that he is a man makes no difference whatsoever."

"Perhaps it doesn't to you. But I have a hunch that Alex would not look at a male publicist the way he looks at you."

"I don't know what you're talking about."

"I'm talking about how often his eyes stray to you during a conversation. He was aware of you all the time we sat there."

"You're imagining things."

"Whatever you say."

"So tell me how you're coming along on the ranch."

At least that topic of conversation worked, and for the rest of the evening they chatted about the ranch, the family, and all their plans.

She didn't have as much trouble telling him about Kent as she had thought she would. Perhaps she had gotten a better perspective on their relationship than she'd consciously realized. Whatever it was, she found it almost painless to explain that she and Kent had decided that what they had was a close friendship, one they both enjoyed, but that marriage was stretching what they felt for each other too far.

Why hadn't she seen that earlier? Meeting Alex Sloan seemed to have opened her eyes to several things she had never truly faced before.

Hours later she lay awake, thinking about her dinner with her brother, recollecting the time she'd spent with Alex, and absently wondering if he was next door. It wasn't all that late, but since Dave needed to fly back that night, they hadn't lingered. Stephanie had thought that getting to bed early was just what she needed, but she had drifted in and out of sleep.

When she heard Alex's door open, Stephanie suddenly recognized what she had been waiting for—she'd been listening for Alex to return. She relaxed, smiling to herself. She was worse than a dorm mother and with less cause. Her eyes drifted closed then popped open at an unexpected sound—a woman's smothered laughter. A low male voice quickly shushed her.

He'd brought a woman with him and he didn't want Stephanie to know. So what? It was nothing to her, after all. She wasn't his keeper.

Stephanie got out of bed and went into the bathroom for a drink of water. Who cared who was with him? It could be Teresa Sinclair. They had certainly been friendly enough during the interview.

What about the number of attractive women who'd been at the autographing? Several had lingered to chat with him. And what difference did it make?

None whatsoever.

Stephanie stomped back to bed and irritably jerked the covers up over her shoulders. With her back to the connecting door she forced herself to concentrate on her breathing, to clear her mind of all thoughts, and to relax. Although she heard nothing more from next door, it was a long time before she fell asleep.

They were on the plane for Seattle two days later before any mention was made of her brother Dave's visit, partly because they had had very little time alone that wasn't taken up with a very busy schedule. In addition, Stephanie was determined not to refer to the night for fear Alex would think she was prying or, even worse, interested in how he had spent his free time.

She had been so preoccupied that the actual take-off had not created as much of a trauma as it generally did. She idly noted that Alex seemed content to relax and enjoy some precious quiet time when no demands were being made on him.

They had left Denver immediately after his luncheon speech for the Veterans of Foreign Wars. Although he had talked about his book, the thrust of his message was to identify himself with those to whom he spoke. Only someone who had experienced war could understand its horrors and his compassionate comments had caused a surge of warmth and appreciation from his audience.

She had had to coax him away from several of the men who were talking with him so that they didn't miss their plane. Neither of them had had much to say since then.

Eventually Alex spoke. "I liked your brother, Stephanie. I haven't had a chance to tell you."

She smiled. "I'm glad. He was very impressed with you, too."

"Once he found out I wasn't sleeping with his sister."

She knew the hateful color betrayed her reaction to his comment. "Brothers tend to be that way."

"How many do you have?"

"Three."

He grinned. "No wonder you learned how to hold your own in a man's world."

She returned his smile. "It helped, believe me."

"I certainly enjoyed seeing Jason again the other night," he continued casually. "We were overseas together, several years ago. Ended up talking until all hours. He and his wife Peggy brought me back to the hotel. I was afraid we'd wake you up."

Stephanie digested that piece of unsolicited information. The woman in his room had been with her husband. Amazing what a difference that made to her.

"I went to bed early that night. My stamina isn't all that I could wish it to be." Her eyes met his for a moment, then darted away. "I never heard you at all," she lied.

"What do we have scheduled when we get into Seattle?" he asked. "Do we have any free time?"

She opened her briefcase and pulled out the rather battered-looking copy of their itinerary. "Nothing until tomorrow."

"Great. I have some friends there I'd like to see. Do you think that would be possible?"

"I don't see why not. The purpose of the tour isn't an endurance or torture test, you know. You can actually enjoy yourself, if you have a mind to do that sort of thing."

He laughed, and she noticed that he seemed to be relaxing for the first time in the last couple of days. Alex was so good at hiding what he was thinking and feeling that she hadn't realized how tense he had been until he started to unwind.

Alex was so pleased to see that Stephanie was smiling and starting to tease him again that he wanted to grab her and kiss her. However, his familiarity with her was what had started the problem in the first place. At least he assumed it was. Ever since her brother had met her, Stephanie had been very aloof, although unfailingly polite.

He had decided it was due to his clumsiness in answering her phone and for kissing her earlier. Although she had graciously received his apology, she had continued to keep her distance. Now she appeared to be loosening up some.

Alex found it unfortunate that he continued to be so aware of her. The longer he was around Stephanie, the more difficult he found it to restrain himself from touching her, kissing her, somehow provoking her into an acknowledgement of what was happening between them.

Five

A steady rain greeted them at Sea-Tac International Airport. Stephanie wasn't surprised. Although the Seattle area was beautifully green and lush, the necessary rain to make it so did not endear itself to her, and she looked out at the moisture with distaste while waiting for Alex to claim their luggage.

Without realizing quite how he had managed to do it, Stephanie had allowed Alex to take control of their traveling arrangements, so now she waited and watched the gray sky as it continued to rain.

"Ready?" he asked, at her elbow. She turned and saw him standing there, a bag in each hand.

"Yes," she said, reaching for her suitcase.

He stepped around her and headed toward the row of taxis waiting outside the door. When they were settled in the back seat of the cab and on their way toward Seattle, Alex glanced out the window. "Does it always rain here?"

"No. Sometimes it's just cloudy and overcast."

"What about the sun?"

"Oh, the sun shines once in a while. Too bad no one ever knows in advance. Just think of the number of people who would flock out here if they knew which days the sun would shine."

"I take it you don't care for the rain."

She grinned. "Oh, it's not so bad, really. The problem is that I'm hopeless with umbrellas. I leave them everywhere I go. And I generally forget to carry a raincoat." She glanced down at the suit she was wearing. "I'm trying to accept the fact that the rain-spattered look may be with me throughout our stay here."

"When do we leave?"

"Tomorrow evening. You have a speech to give this evening, a morning talk show on television, and an autographing right after lunch."

"Who planned this schedule, anyway?"

"I did, why?"

"Didn't you ever think we'd want some time to re-lax and maybe see some of the sights?"

She eyed him warily. "It never occurred to me. Your agent made it clear that you had very little time. I didn't think you would want it taken up with sight-seeing tours."

He sighed. "An occasionally relaxing meal might be nice, though."

"True. We'll be spending the weekend in San Francisco. I don't think there's anything planned for Sunday afternoon or evening."

"Good. May I take you to dinner at Fisherman's Wharf on Sunday?"

She glanced at him in surprise. He sounded so serious. "If you'd like," she replied. "Although I'd think that you'd want some time away from me. We've been practically inseparable since we met in Philadelphia."

"Oh, I don't know. I can think of a few things we haven't done together."

He wore the utmost innocent expression she'd ever seen. How could she possibly take exception to his statement when she wasn't sure what he was referring to? The trouble was she wasn't absolutely certain she wanted to find out, either. But her curiosity won out over her discretion.

"Such as?"

He gazed out the window for a moment. Then he glanced at her and said, "We haven't seen a movie together, or gone to a symphony, much less a ball game. There are several more things I could mention, but you get the general idea."

"You're right. I would have had some difficulty working all of those into our rather tight schedule."

"Nevertheless, I'd like to do all of them with you sometime."

"Why?"

"Why? I thought that was obvious by now. I want to get to know you better, Stephanie. I'm sure I'm not telling you anything you don't already know when I say that I'm very attracted to you."

Stephanie could no longer meet his gaze. She turned her head and gazed out the taxi window, relieved to see the skyline of Seattle before them.

"Alex, I can't—I mean, you mustn't— That is, the reason that—" She stopped speaking, knowing that she wasn't making a great deal of sense.

"What is it?"

Forcing herself to look at him, she said, "I think you should know that since Christmas I've been making plans to be married this summer."

Alex felt as though a giant fist had socked him somewhere in his stomach. He glanced down at her hands held tightly together in her lap. "You aren't wearing a ring," he offered quietly. "I'm afraid I didn't realize your circumstances."

"I returned it two weeks ago."

His heart suddenly took on a burst of lightness, and Alex was hard put not to break into a big grin. However, he knew that sort of reaction was inappropriate. Obviously, what she had gone through was disturbing. "I see," he offered guardedly.

"That relationship has occupied my personal life for the past four years. Before that I didn't have much time for a personal life." She glanced up, her eyes a beautiful, liquid blue. "What I'm trying to say is, I don't have much experience dating men, and particularly not someone like you."

He found himself tensing at her qualification. "What do you mean, someone like me?"

"Experienced, traveled. I'm sure the women you know are considerably more sophisticated than I am, more aware of what is expected of them."

"I don't expect anything from you that you don't freely wish to give. I would be honored to be offered your friendship. I would treasure it."

His gentle tone and soft words brought a lump to her throat. They drew up in front of their hotel in silence.

Alex paid the driver and handed their luggage over to the hotel attendant while Stephanie walked over to the reservations desk. Within a short time they were signed in.

"How much time do we have?" Alex asked, appearing by her shoulder.

She glanced at her watch. "A car is supposed to pick us up at seven."

"Then we have a little time. Why don't we explore downtown Seattle? We don't have to go far."

"In this rain?"

"We'll find an umbrella. Come on. I'd like to get some fresh air."

The idea sounded appealing. Alex seemed more relaxed, somehow, as though saying what he had in the taxi had given him a sense of freedom. Glancing down at her clothes, Stephanie said, "If we're going walking in the rain, I want to find something more suitable to wear."

Alex took her arm. "Then let's go upstairs so you can change."

Once again their rooms were connected. The accommodations were luxurious, and Stephanie gave a silent thanks to whoever had recommended that they stay in this particular hotel. She felt pampered.

Opening her suitcase, she quickly found a pair of slacks and low-heeled shoes. Within minutes she was changed. She tapped on the connecting door. Alex opened it and pulled her into his room.

"Just look at this view," he said, tugging her toward the window.

The rain had stopped and the sky was beginning to clear. From their high vantage point, they could see out across the water to some distant islands. A large ferry was moving toward shore while another one pulled away, heading toward the peninsula. A light mist was rapidly dissipating as the sun attempted to break from behind the clouds lining the western horizon.

Alex dropped his arm companionably around her shoulders. "What do you think?"

"It's truly beautiful, isn't it?"

When he didn't answer her she glanced at him and discovered that he was looking at her with a warm expression. "Yes. Truly beautiful," he murmured.

As though he could no longer resist the temptation, Alex slid his other arm around her and pulled her closer to him. Then he kissed her. His kiss caught her off guard with its intensity. He seemed hungry for her as his mouth explored the contours of hers. Stephanie knew somewhere in the back of her mind that she shouldn't be allowing this to happen. They were business acquaintances, nothing more. They should not be getting involved with each other.

The only problem was, they were already involved, regardless of whether they expressed what they were feeling or refused to give in to what was obviously happening between them. She felt herself relax against him, her body fitting to his as though she had been designed to mesh perfectly with his tall, muscled figure.

His tongue gently nudged her mouth open, and Stephanie felt as though he had taken possession of her when it darted between her lips to intimately touch and tease her.

She wrapped her arms tightly around his waist, aware of how he was responding to her closeness, but no longer caring. What she was feeling at the moment was too new, too exciting, too appealing for her to be concerned with the consequences of what was happening between them. It was time to enjoy the experience.

When he finally raised his head they were both breathing in short, panting gasps.

"My God, what you do to me," he finally managed to say. He held her against his chest and took long, deep breaths. "We'd better get out of here. Now."

He let her go, took her hand and they left his room.

Stephanie knew that if he hadn't been leading her down the hallway and into the elevator, it was quite possible she would have walked into walls and doors. She still wasn't sure what had happened to her. She could only liken it to having a pile of bricks suddenly falling on her head.

She felt dazed and disoriented.

By the time they were out on the street, a pale sunlight had brightened the day considerably. Stephanie allowed Alex to take the lead. They explored the downtown area, including Pike's Market, and stepped into one of the shops across the street for coffee.

"Don't you want to try some of the pastries?" he asked, nodding toward the display case that was filled with mouth-watering confections.

"I would love to, but if I ate things like those, I wouldn't be able to wear any of the clothes I brought with me."

He glanced down at the slacks that covered her trim figure. "I can see nothing wrong with the way your clothes fit."

Darn it, she wished she would not color in reaction to his words. He had a way of speaking to her that suggested a much greater intimacy than any they had ever shared. Anyone seeing them together would assume they were lovers. She'd never had anyone treat her that way, not even Kent.

Alex gave the impression that he was only barely restraining himself from sweeping her up and carrying her off to bed. The thought of such an action created a tingle that ran through her.

Glancing at her watch, Stephanie reluctantly said, "I really think we need to get back to the hotel."

Alex stood and held her chair for her. "Whatever you say."

When they arrived back at their rooms, Alex opened her door for her, then went into his own without comment. Stephanie felt as though she needed some breathing space. The man's presence was certainly potent. She really needed to keep her wits about her. He couldn't help having the charismatic personality that seemed to draw all women to him, but she was having more and more difficulty maintaining her sensible attitude about men in general and clients in particular.

After a long shower, accompanied by an even longer lecture to herself about her priorities, Stephanie got on the phone and spoke to the coordinator for that night's appearance. She discovered that the books that had been ordered and scheduled to arrive days ago, had just come in an hour ago. Once again, Stephanie realized that this way of life was more conducive to ulcers and high blood pressure than anything else.

Her mind was still on their schedule when she heard Alex's tap on the connecting door. Absently calling for him to enter, she reached for the phone, only to forget what she was doing when he walked through the door.

He wore a stark black suit, which contrasted with the pristine white of his dress shirt. The suit seemed to emphasize his tall, erect figure, causing his shoulders to look even wider than usual, his waist more narrow, his hips and thighs more muscular.

In short, he was devastating. And this was the man she had just resolved not to respond to anymore.

Fat chance.

Alex forgot what he was going to say as soon as he walked into the room. Stephanie sat on the side of the bed near the phone. Her silver-blond hair gleamed in the soft lamplight. Her eyes were deeply shadowed by her luxuriantly long lashes, and he caught a hint of vulnerability in her expression.

He wanted to take her in his arms and reassure her somehow. He was just as surprised at what was happening between them as she was, but he wasn't fighting it. What he felt for this woman was too strong to fight. He understood that he would have to go slow. She was recovering from a broken engagement, the details of which she hadn't shared with him, but it was obvious she had not taken the matter lightly.

The dress she wore was soft and flowing, yet businesslike. Of course, Alex was convinced that she would look graceful and alluring in a sack, but he recognized more than a touch of prejudice in his thinking.

"Are you ready?" he finally asked as the silence between them continued.

"Oh! Uh, yes. I was just going to—" She paused and looked at the phone as though hoping to find an answer. Finally, she shrugged. "It doesn't matter." Coming to her feet she picked up her bag and said, "We might as well go down and wait for the car."

He escorted her downstairs as though she were the most precious thing in his life. Alex was beginning to discover that there was more than a grain of truth in the thought.

It was almost midnight by the time they returned to their rooms. Once again Stephanie was made aware of the keen intelligence and charismatic presence of the man with whom she traveled.

The dinner was well attended, and Alex made a riveting, compelling speech. Then he fielded some tough questions with his customary aplomb. After the activities were concluded, he was once again surrounded by people who wanted to speak to him, offer invitations, and continue to probe into sensitive matters.

Stephanie stayed in the background, waiting, until Alex excused himself from the group and came striding over to where she stood. "I'm sorry to keep you waiting," he said, taking her arm.

She smiled. "That's part of my job. I'm really pleased with the number of people who obviously heard about your tour and wanted to meet you." She glanced down at his hand. "Getting writer's cramp yet from signing so many books?"

He slid his hand to the nape of her neck and gently pulled her against him. "Let's just say I don't really think I could spend much of my time doing this type of thing."

The limousine that had brought them to the dinner waited outside for them. Once they were seated within it, Stephanie said, "I'm really surprised. You are so good at public appearances. I would have guessed that you'd done it for years."

"No."

"Then what do you do?"

He glanced at her. "Now?"

She shrugged. "Anytime. What have your duties been?"

He glanced at the driver in front of them. "It's a rather long and boring story. Someday when we have more time I'll tell you."

And he meant it. If he was going to have a relationship with this woman, and he fully intended to have one, then he would need to be as open and candid with her as possible. Alex was surprised to discover that in a few short days his perspective regarding his life had changed.

Making a commitment to another person no longer seemed to be a burden. With Stephanie it would become a pleasure. There was so much he wanted to share with her, so many things that would help her to understand who he was and why he had become the type of person he was.

When they reached their rooms, Alex opened her door for her and paused. "I'm going to tell you good night here. It's safer." Then he took her in his arms and kissed her.

There was no resistance from Stephanie. Not now. She had faced several things tonight as she'd sat and watched Alex, not the least of which was her feelings for the man. She had stopped fighting them. Who knew where any of this would lead? All she knew was that she felt too strongly to deny those feelings any longer.

When Alex finally loosened his hold on her, she was flushed and breathless. He found her adorable. She was like no other woman he'd ever known or hoped to meet.

"Good night," he whispered. He waited until she closed and locked her door before going into his own room.

Stephanie felt as though she floated into her room. Why had she fought so hard? This marvelous feeling made everything worthwhile. Dreamily, she undressed, showered and slipped into her gown. When she fell asleep her thoughts were about Alex.

When she awakened her thoughts were disoriented. She'd been dreaming—a marvelous, truly sensuous dream—when something disturbed her. Forcing herself awake she lay there for a moment and realized that what she was hearing was a soft chiming in the room. She glanced around, trying to figure out where it was coming from.

The sound was reminiscent of the soft chime elevators made when they reached a floor, but this noise continued on a regular cycle. Stephanie reached for the lamp and turned it on, then glanced at her watch. It was only a little after two o'clock in the morning!

Had someone set the alarm on the clock radio there by the bed? She squinted, trying to read the dial. Then a clear, disembodied voice spoke in a calm, soothing tone.

"A smoke alarm has been activated in the hotel. Please do not open your door. Check the map on the back of the door to verify where the closest fire escape is located. Please remain in your room until further notice. The cause of the alarm is being investigated, and we will continue to keep you informed of the situation."

The voice stopped, but the irritating little chime continued to sound every few seconds. Stephanie was stunned, trying to take in what was happening. A fire? A fire here in the hotel?

The faint sound of a siren could be heard in the distance, and she seemed to be jolted into sudden awareness.

A fire!

She threw back the covers and lunged out of the bed just as the connecting door swung open and Alex burst into the room.

"Are you awake?" he demanded, coming over to her.

"How could anyone sleep through that noise?" she complained, pushing her hair away from her face. She vaguely noticed that Alex was wearing a pair of jeans that were zipped but not buttoned. His chest was bare.

"You need to get dressed," he said, striding over to her suitcase and trying to ignore how alluring she looked in her thigh-length gown, tousled hair and sleepy expression.

"So do you," she pointed out, staring down at his bare feet. "Besides, they told us not to leave." She could feel the adrenaline racing through her system. Her heart pounded in her chest, and the thought occurred to her that she could very easily die before the night was out!

How could this be happening? She felt as though she were in some sort of nightmarish state. Nothing was real. Not her, and not the man standing there watching her as though looking for signs of panic.

"Yes, I know we're to stay in our rooms, but we need to be ready to leave, just in case." Alex continued to watch her, waiting to see how she was going to react.

When he saw that she obediently went to her suitcase and began to pull out some clothes, he went into the bathroom, gathered all the towels there and threw them into the tub. Then he began to run water on them.

Stephanie knew that she was fighting panic. The steady chiming of the bell wasn't helping to calm her nerves. Why didn't someone shut it off?

She heard Alex in her bathroom and peeked through the open doorway. "Isn't this a rather strange time to decide to take a bath?" she asked, wondering if he realized what he was doing.

Once the towels were soaked, he turned the water off and walked back into the bedroom. She had pulled on a pair of slacks, and as he watched, she slipped a long sleeved shirt over her gown. He didn't comment on her actions. Instead, he answered her question. "I wanted to have some wet towels ready in case we have to leave the room. They would be some protection for us." He glanced around the room, taking in everything in a moment. "I'll be right back," he said, disappearing into the other room, "as soon as I finish dressing."

Somehow his actions made what was happening seem more real, and Stephanie started to tremble. What was going to happen to them? All at once her schedule, her profession, her life-style seemed to diminish in importance, as she took in the fact that her life was being threatened and she was helpless to know what to do.

She had always prided herself on being in control—of herself, of the situation in which she might find herself, wherever she might be. For the first time she recognized what an illusion being in control really was. Too many things could happen where a person had no option but to accept.

The waiting for information was even worse. What were they supposed to do? If they were to be evacuated, could they take their luggage? Was there anything here that she couldn't live without?

She glanced around when Alex came back. He walked over to the window and looked out, but there was nothing to see but the night. They were too high to see the street directly below them.

The soft voice came on once again, still soothing, repeating most of the earlier message. When the message was concluded, Stephanie wandered over and stood beside Alex at the window, staring out at the night. "How bad do you think it is?" she finally asked, dismayed to hear the quaver in her voice.

He shrugged. "Who knows? Even if the lobby were in flames they would be giving the same message. We're probably in the safest place we could be at the moment."

"Oh, I don't know," Stephanie managed to say with a lightness she was far from feeling. "Walking along the beach seems considerably safer to me."

"I meant in the hotel," he said with a grin. "As far as the beach, how can you tell? A giant tidal wave could come along and suddenly sweep you off your feet.''

''You're a real bundle of encouragement, aren't you?'' she pointed out, making a face.

At least she wasn't alone. In fact, Stephanie realized that if she had to be going through such a nightmarish experience she could think of no one with whom she'd rather be.

Alex exuded a sense of quiet confidence, a take-charge attitude that she found immensely reassuring for some reason. If he was nervous, it didn't show. Alex appeared alert and ready for action, and yet somehow he managed to convey the impression that he was relaxed and at ease.

She wished that she knew how he did it. Any minute now, she felt as though she was going to break into hysterical laughter. Here she was with an extremely attractive male in her hotel room, at two o'clock in the morning, and all she could think about was that she was on the verge of making a complete fool of herself.

Alex could feel Stephanie's tension and understood it. She had probably never been in a situation so serious before, where no immediate action could be taken to relieve the pent-up nervousness. He had lived so much of his life under similar circumstances that he was having no problem dealing with the pumped-up energy that flowed throughout his body.

He knew he was going to have to do something or she was going to fall to pieces. In fact, he felt a tremendous sense of pride in the way she'd handled herself up until now.

Turning to her, Alex pointed to the pair of chairs grouped around the table near the wide window. "Why don't we sit down?" he suggested, pulling out one of the chairs. "I'll tell you about my friend, Steve."

Stephanie glanced around. "Why not? There doesn't seem to be much else we can do at the moment. I certainly can't see us trying to go back to sleep!"

Once again the voice came on and quietly recited the same message—reassuring the listeners that everything was under control.

Stephanie got this sudden vision of a tape recorder playing over and over in front of a microphone in an empty lobby while the hotel personnel scrambled for safety. Then she shook her head. She had to get a grip on herself. Her imagination was working overtime.

She sat down in the chair and Alex sat across from her. Cocking his head slightly, he said, "That constant chime could slowly drive you round the bend, couldn't it?"

"You're telling me. I wish they'd turn it off."

"The hotel personnel want you to be aware that you are in communication with them. By hearing the continuous sound, you are supposed to be reassured."

"Then how about something more commercial, like the top twenty hits or something?"

"At two o'clock in the morning?" he asked, feigning dismay. "Please spare us!"

She leaned back in her chair. "So tell me about Steve," she suggested, forcing herself to become resigned to the steady accompaniment coming over the hidden speaker in the room. Stephanie found that she was truly interested in hearing more about Alex and his friend, hoping to learn more about the man she was with.

Alex's expression grew softer as he began to speak. "Steve McCormick and I met at the Academy, in Colorado Springs, years ago." He began to reminisce, and like the fabled storytellers of old, he began to weave a magic spell for Stephanie. Slowly she began to relax as she got caught up in his anecdotes about the scrapes and shared experiences. Alex talked about the funny times, and there were many of those because of Steve's crazy sense of humor, and the more serious times when each of them had been there for the other one—when Alex's mother had died, and later, when Steve's father was killed.

She realized that they were closer than brothers, these two only children. Theirs was a lifelong friendship and they treasured it.

At one point, Alex paused and quietly said, "Steve was best man at my wedding. Two years later I was best man at his."

Stephanie blinked. Nothing in Alex's biography indicated that he had ever been married. Not that she should have been surprised. He was too attractive not to have been involved with more than one woman in his past, even though his bio stated that he was single and had no children.

How did he feel about that? Was he filled with regret or pleased that he didn't have the responsibilities inherent in a family?

There was so much about this man that she wanted to know.

In a level voice that was carefully devoid of all expression, Alex went on, "About a year ago, Steve was involved in a military plane crash that killed several of the crew and severely injured the ones who survived."

Stephanie sat up. "Oh, no! How horrible. What happened to him?"

"He received multiple injuries and was told he would never be able to walk again, but he refuses to accept that diagnosis. He went through a period of operations and physical therapy that would have done in a lesser man."

They were quiet for several minutes. Once again the message came over the intercom that the cause of the fire alarm was being investigated, that they were to stay in their rooms and wait for further instruction.

Somehow the repetition of the same message lent it credibility, made it seem reassuring. Whatever was happening, it was being taken care of. All they could do was wait.

She glanced at Alex who was leaning back in the well-padded chair, his legs stretched out in front of him, his gaze fixed on the tip of his shoes.

Was he thinking of Steve? Or was he thinking about being stuck in a hotel room while a fire might be raging somewhere close by? She couldn't tell.

He glanced up at her and gave her a half smile that she found very endearing. Without thinking she returned his smile.

"Where is Steve now?" she finally asked.

"He's at a rehab center in Virginia. I try to visit him a couple of times a month when I can. Sometimes that's not possible, but he understands."

"What about his wife? Is she able to visit regularly? And his children. Does he have any children?"

"A son who lives with his mother in California. Steve hasn't seen him in several years."

"That's too bad. I take it he's divorced."

"Yes. Military life is tough on marriages. We both found that out the hard way."

"How much longer will he be at the center?"

"No one knows at this point. I'd like to say that the worst seems to be behind him, but sometimes it's hard to say. He's been battling with this thing for a long time and he's tired. I worry about him, about his morale."

He paused because another announcement came on. "The smoke alarm that was activated has been investigated. The problem has been corrected. Thank you for your patience during this time."

Blessed silence ensued after the final words, and Alex and Stephanie looked at each other in surprise. They had actually grown used to the constant sound. Now the silence seemed almost strange.

Stephanie began to laugh, the relief that was flooding through her making her almost weak. "That was it? The fire is over?" she finally managed to ask.

"Looks that way," he replied. Alex got up and walked over to her door. He opened it and glanced out into the hallway. Several other people were doing the same thing and acting sheepish when they were seen. A babble of conversation and relieved laughter echoed down the hallway, and Alex closed the door and locked it, then turned back to Stephanie.

"Looks like the excitement is over for the night. We might as well go back to bed." He walked over to her and gently touched her cheek. "In case you're wondering where you put your nightgown, you're still wearing it."

She glanced down self-consciously. It didn't show beneath her slacks and shirt, but she realized what she must have done and gave him an embarrassed smile. She stood and found herself only a few inches away from him.

"Thank you for keeping me company. I appreciate it more than I can possibly say."

"I didn't want to spend the time alone, myself," he admitted.

A different sort of tension seemed to be filling the room, and once again Stephanie became aware of the peculiar isolation that comes from being alone with someone at that time of the morning.

She found herself rushing into speech in order to mask the pulsating silence around them. "You're probably used to emergency alerts and things of that nature."

"I may be used to them, but I've never grown to like them," he admitted with a slight smile.

Alex leaned over the necessary distance between them and kissed her softly on the lips. "Good night, Stephanie. Sweet dreams."

His gentle kiss further rattled her. "I hope I don't dream of fires and sirens," she said, laughing nervously.

He slipped his arms around her and hugged her to
him. His kiss this time was more leisurely and considerably more thorough. Stephanie could feel her restraints slipping away while she clung to him and
returned his kiss.

The next thing she was aware of was his lowering her
to the bed while they continued to kiss. Now that she
was beside him, she no longer had to concentrate on
keeping enough control of her legs to hold her weight.
Instead, she could concentrate all her senses on
touching him, exploring the broad expanse of his
shoulders and the way his torso narrowed so beguil-
ingly at the waist.

Stephanie gave an unconscious moan, and Alex realized what was happening. They were on the bed together in the early hours of the morning. Their
defenses were down and they were obviously enjoying
being together.

But how would Stephanie feel about the situation in
the morning? They had both been tense, too keyed up
to handle the tension without some sort of release. He
already knew the aphrodisiacal effects danger had on
a person.

But did Stephanie? And could he take advantage of
the situation? If all he wanted was a brief interlude to
be forgotten by daylight, he would not have hesi-
tated. But Alex wanted so much more from Stephanie.

He never wanted to be accused of taking advantage
of their situation.

But how could he leave her when she was so relaxed and loving in his arms?

He opened his eyes and looked down at her. Even while he had been questioning the wisdom of what was happening, he'd unbuttoned and removed her blouse so that she was clad in her nightgown and slacks. His hand caressed her breasts, loving the feel of them, the fullness, their response to his touch.

"I want to make love to you," he whispered, his mouth searching for and finding that vulnerable spot just below her ear.

His words jolted her out of a hazy world of sensation and pleasure. She was enjoying his kisses, his caresses, his— Her eyes flew open, and Stephanie realized where they were and what they were doing.

"No," she managed to say. "We can't," she added, trying to bring herself out of the fog his kiss had created around her.

"I was afraid you'd say that," he said with a smile, then sat up on the bed beside her. "In that case, I'd better get out of here, fast."

She stared up at him, bewildered at his lack of argument. He didn't even seem angry, or frustrated, even though she was fully aware of his arousal.

"You aren't angry, are you?" she asked.

He shook his head. "No. We're only postponing the inevitable. We both know it. I want you in my bed, Stephanie, but when the time comes I want to know it's through your choice and not because of the circumstances."

He leaned over and gave her a quick kiss. "I'll see you in a few hours for breakfast." Alex left her side and went into the other room, closing the door between them.

Stephanie couldn't believe what had almost happened just now. What she had wanted to happen. What Alex pointed out was going to happen... sooner or later.

She couldn't find a convincing argument against his logic. For the first time since she could remember, Stephanie was frightened, not of another person, but of her own feelings.

She was in love with Colonel Alexander E. Sloan. She must be out of her mind.

Six

——

When the alarm went off the next morning, Stephanie was convinced she had just closed her eyes. She didn't know what time she had finally gone back to sleep, but it couldn't have been more than an hour or two before the alarm had been set to go off.

They had to be at the television studio by eight.

Dragging herself out of bed, she stumbled into the bathroom only to discover all of her bath towels soaking in the tub. Groaning, she began to wring them out and hang them around the bathroom to dry.

Still half asleep, she went over and tapped on Alex's door. When he opened the door she saw that he had already showered, if the dampness of his hair was any indication, and was clad in his slacks. She ignored his look of surprise. "The least you can do is loan me the use of one of your towels," she greeted him, "since you so conscientiously soaked all of mine last night."

Without saying a word he walked into his bathroom and came back carrying a neatly folded towel. "Good morning to you, too," he offered with a grin.

She shook her head. "I'm sorry to be such a grouch. I just don't feel like I got much sleep last night."

"You didn't. We didn't get the all-clear signal until after four. And it's only a few minutes past six now."

"I suppose that should make me feel better, but at the moment the thought doesn't particularly console me."

He leaned against the door frame and took in her rumpled appearance. "You know, you could stay here and sleep, if you'd like. I can meet you here after the television interview."

She looked at him in horror. "Are you serious? What sort of a publicist would I be if I were to let my clients go to all their interviews and meetings without me?"

"A sleepy one, perhaps?"

"You didn't get any more sleep than I did. How are you able to look so rested and alert?"

He smiled, amused at her irritation. She looked like a ruffled kitten trying to decide whom to attack. Her eyes were heavy-lidded and more seductive than she could have guessed.

"Because I'm used to going on limited amounts of sleep," he explained gently. Straightening from his lounging position, he carefully turned her around so that she was facing her bathroom. "Now, then, if you want to come with me, I would suggest you get a move on. I don't know about you, but I'm starved. I didn't get much to eat last night."

Stephanie nodded and turned away, too tired to take exception to his air of command. When she glanced into the bathroom mirror she flinched. There were deep circles under her eyes, and her skin was pale. She also realized that she hadn't bothered to put on her robe before getting a towel from Alex.

"I must be losing my mind," she muttered, slipping out of her gown and turning on the water. She quickly grabbed the complimentary shower cap and pulled it over her head. There was no time to do more than brush her hair before leaving.

Later, after they had ordered breakfast in the hotel coffee shop and were sipping their coffee, Alex said, "You did a great job of getting ready this morning. I didn't think you'd manage."

The reviving coffee was doing wonders for her. She could actually smile at his gentle teasing. "I can't let you think you're the only one who can function in an emergency." After sipping from her cup again, she added, "I'm just glad I'm not the one being interviewed this morning."

"It's not so bad, really. Everyone asks about the same questions. I've had relatively few surprises."

She finally decided to ask him the question that had popped into her head more than once that morning, particularly after the scare they'd had the night before.

"Are you eager to get back to Washington?"

"Not really," he responded, as though surprised. "I've rather enjoyed the trip." He reached over and took her hand. "Of course, the company has been exceptionally pleasant, as well, but I've also enjoyed meeting people that are in no way connected with the military."

Feeling a sense of ease with him that was new, Stephanie asked another personal question that she'd wondered about.

"Do you expect to write any more, or was this just something that you felt you needed to express and now that the book has been published, you're content to continue with your old way of life?"

"Actually, I have another book about half-completed. I find that I enjoy the change of pace that writing offers. Of course, there are times when I have no available time to write, but when I do, it's become very peaceful to me."

She took another sip of coffee and said, "You certainly didn't choose a very peaceful subject to write about for your first book. Is the second one anything like it?"

"Not much, no. But I suppose you can find similarities if you look for them."

"How long do you intend to stay in the service?"

He smiled, amused at her interrogation, but more than willing to answer her. He was encouraged that she was showing so much interest in his plans for the future. "I don't suppose I've ever given it much thought. It's what I do...the way I live...my profession. I suppose I'll stay in the military until I feel that I've accomplished what I set out to accomplish."

"And what is that?"

He was quiet while the waiter placed their meals in front of them. After the waiter left, Alex picked up his refilled cup and drank. "Anything I would say sounds corny, I'm afraid. It's just that I feel very privileged to have been born in this country, to have received the benefits that a country based on our many freedoms offers. I wanted to make sure that those born after me would be able to enjoy those same freedoms."

"That's not corny at all," she said quietly.

"It's a rather flag-waving attitude that's a little unpopular with some of our population."

"That's because so many of us tend to take what we have for granted without realizing how easily and quickly we could lose our way of life."

"Yes, because so few people have seen any other way of life. When you've lived in as many countries as I have over the years, and been involved with as many military actions, you can better appreciate what we have here at home."

They were quiet as they quickly finished their breakfasts and left for the television studio.

While Stephanie waited for Alex to complete the interview, her thoughts kept returning to their breakfast conversation. Regardless of what he had seen or suffered, Alex still maintained his idealism regarding his profession. She continued to discover surprising facets to his personality and a depth of character that fascinated her.

She almost groaned aloud at the realization that she had been hoping to find something about him that would diminish the attraction she felt for him. In-

stead, she kept uncovering more and more characteristics about him that touched her very deeply.

When they returned to the hotel to get their luggage and check out, Stephanie was surprised to find
that she had a message to call Kent. She looked at it in
dismay. Why would he be calling her in Seattle?

She excused herself to Alex once they got to their
rooms and told him she would meet him downstairs in
a few minutes. Then she went inside and returned the
call. When Kent's secretary put her call through immediately, even though she explained that he was in a
meeting, Stephanie was even more puzzled.

"Hi, Steph, how's it going?" he asked in a friendly
tone when he picked up the receiver.

"Fine. Why did you call, Kent?"

"Just found out a couple of hours ago that I have
to be in San Francisco first thing Monday. Thought I
might fly out tomorrow if you thought you'd have
some time to see me."

Kent wanted to see her? Why? They hadn't seen
each other in almost three weeks, and their phone calls
had been stilted and awkward.

"I'm not sure, Kent. The Saturday schedule is
rather hectic. I don't think we get a break until Sunday afternoon."

"That will work out fine with me. Why don't I meet
you at your hotel about two o'clock on Sunday." He
paused, then said, "I really want to see you, Steph.
Would you do that for me?"

She could hear emotion in his voice that he was
fighting to restrain. Something was wrong, but there

was no way for her to know what, not unless she agreed to see him.

"All right, Kent. I'll see you then."

"Thank you, love. This is really important to me."

She hung up the phone and glanced at her watch. They needed to be on their way to the airport within the hour. Hastily checking her room for any forgotten item, Stephanie grabbed her bag and walked out the door, only to find Alex waiting patiently in the hallway.

"I thought you had gone downstairs."

He reached over and took her bag from her unresisting fingers, picked up his own and started down the hallway. "Bad news?" he asked.

"Uh, no. At least I don't think so. I made an appointment for Sunday afternoon."

"Does that mean our dinner at Fisherman's Wharf will have to be postponed?"

She smiled. "Not at all. I'm looking forward to it."

"So am I," he said, stepping into the elevator behind her.

During the next couple of days, Stephanie had reason to wonder more than once why Kent needed to see her so urgently. What had happened to him? She realized that she cared about him and his happiness in the same way she would have cared for one of her brothers.

What an interesting revelation that was. Had she always confused her feelings for him that way? What had made her think that what she felt for Kent was what was needed between a husband and wife?

And what had happened to her to make her recognize there was a difference? She didn't have to look too far to find the answers to her questions. Alexander Sloan and all of the feelings he evoked within her—that's what had happened. Now she could feel concern for Kent without feeling personally involved.

How interesting. And how revealing.

By the time they returned to their hotel in San Francisco on Saturday night, Stephanie was ready to crawl into bed. Alex had been quiet—even more quiet than usual—since they had left Seattle.

When they arrived at the hotel, Alex surprised her by suggesting that they go into the lounge and listen to the music, have a drink, and perhaps relax by dancing once or twice.

Stephanie might be tired but she wasn't dead, and she knew that would be the only condition that would prevent her from accepting his offer. Later, as they listened to the music, she wasn't sorry that she had taken the time to change into something more social and less businesslike for this time with Alex.

There was a good crowd there, which was no doubt typical for San Francisco on a Saturday night. She was glad they only had to go upstairs when they were ready to leave. She wondered how far some of these people had to drive to get home and what condition they would be in by that time. Several were feeling the effects of their drinks.

In fact, one fellow had already come over and asked her to dance, ignoring Alex completely. When she politely declined the offer, Alex enforced her words by taking her hand and leading her to the dance floor himself.

She smiled to herself as she leaned her head against his chest, giving herself up to the slow rhythmic beat of the music.

"I didn't realize you enjoyed dancing, Colonel."

"I don't. But it was the only way I could think of to hold you in my arms without getting my face slapped."

She lifted her head so that she could see his face. His eyes were twinkling with a devilish light. "I can recall a few occasions when you didn't seem to be concerned about such a reaction," she pointed out primly.

"I think I've learned some discretion since then. At least I hope so."

They danced in silence, but both were very much aware of the other one. The crowded dance floor kept them pressed close to each other, and both of them recognized the other's reaction.

When the song ended they went back to the table in silence. Alex picked up his drink and drained it, then signaled the waiter for another one.

"Stephanie, I know this isn't the time or place to bring this up, but I want you to know that I've never wanted anyone in my life the way I want you, and it's driving me crazy, being around you constantly, sharing such intimate living arrangements. I think I'm going to go out of my mind."

He shook his head and looked at the dancers who were filling the dance floor once again as a fast-paced song was introduced.

"I'm having the same problem, Alex," she responded quietly, studying her drink as though she would find some answers for them.

"What are we going to do about it?"

She looked at him after a brief hesitation and asked, "What do you want to do about it?"

He grinned. "Take you upstairs and make love to you for the rest of the weekend."

"And after that, we're supposed to forget what happened?"

He shook his head. "No, of course not."

"I tried to tell you, Alex. I'm not the kind to get involved in love affairs. Maybe I've spent too many years being responsible for other people and looking after their concerns. Whatever it is, I can't forget that I owe myself some responsible behavior, as well."

Alex took her hand and held it. "I was married once, for almost nine years. And it didn't work out."

"Why?"

He was quiet for several moments. "Because I didn't spend enough time with her. All of my energy and concentration was directed toward my work."

"And now?"

"What do you mean?"

"If you had a relationship in your life now, would your energy and concentration still be directed toward your work?" She picked up her drink and sipped it, her eyes wary.

He studied her, a puzzled expression on his face. "I don't know. Perhaps not. Why do you ask?"

"Because we all have choices in life, and we don't have to make the same choices every time a similar situation arises. How old were you when you got married?"

"Twenty-five."

"And how old are you now?"

"Forty-three."

"Do you have the same attitudes and perspective as you did then?"

"No."

"In other words, you're not the same person who got married at twenty-five."

"Not really, no."

"Then you have no idea how you would handle marriage now, do you, Colonel?" She glanced around and noticed that another slow song was beginning. "Care to dance?" she asked.

He followed her out to the dance floor and hungrily reached for her as soon as she turned toward him. She flowed into his arms as though that was where she belonged. Alex was rapidly concluding that that was exactly where she belonged. Forever.

"Stephanie?"

"Hmm?"

"I know we haven't known each other long, but—"

"Actually, we'll be celebrating our anniversary tomorrow," she pointed out dryly. "One week."

"I know this sounds crazy, but I can't stand the thought of you disappearing out of my life when this tour is over, and I was wondering if—"

He paused and she glanced up at him. "Are you asking me to go steady, by any chance?"

"No, dammit! Even before your timely lecture about marriage I've been trying to find a way to tell you how I feel. I want to marry you, but I know we haven't known each other long enough to convince you that it would work for us. And I'm frustrated with searching for a reason that would convince you to give some consideration to the idea."

"Oh, I don't know. Loving you is a rather convincing reason, don't you think?"

He stopped dead, causing two different couples to run into them. Then he took her hand and led her from the dance floor. Stopping only long enough at their table to make sure their drinks had been paid for and to leave a tip, Alex continued to lead her out of the room and into the hotel lobby.

"Did I just hear what I thought I heard?"

She glanced around at the deserted lobby, looked at her watch, and headed toward the elevators. "I really think we'd better turn in, don't you? You have that autographing session at eleven in the morning."

"Stephanie!"

She looked at the man who had turned her life upside down in one short week and smiled tenderly at him. "Yes, Colonel?"

The elevator door opened and she stepped inside. He followed her, punched the button for their floor and said, "Did I understand you to say that you love me?"

She sighed. "Crazy, isn't it? Do you suppose it's curable, or am I letting myself in for a lifelong condition?"

He dragged her into his arms and hugged her to him. "I can't believe this," he muttered. "You little wretch. Do you know how much I've been suffering these past few days? Especially after your severe lecture about mixing your professional life with your personal life."

She pushed away from him. "I meant it, Alex. As long as you're my client, that's all I want between us."

The doors of the elevator opened silently and he escorted her into the hallway.

"Perhaps after we finish the tour...go back East..." Her voice trailed off as Stephanie realized that he was not paying any attention to what she was saying. Instead, he had taken her hand and was leading her toward their rooms.

"Alex, listen to me..." she began.

"I'm listening," he replied calmly as he released her long enough to open the door to his room. Then he took her hand once more and led her inside. He closed and locked the door.

"Alex, I—"

Without speaking he stopped by the side of his bed and turned to her. Cupping her face in his hands, he kissed her gently on the mouth. "Stephanie...I understand your principles and admire them greatly. I love you for them. Now, then. Just hush and let me love you."

His mouth found hers once more and she was transported from the situation in which they found themselves. She loved this man. She couldn't explain how it had happened, or why. There was no rhyme or reason to what she was experiencing, but as he held her

closely and kissed her as though he were letting go of
the restraints that had kept him forcibly bound,
Stephanie forgot that she was a publicist and he was an
author, that they were together to promote his book.
She forgot everything but the moment.

Her dress seemed to disappear from between them
as he urgently removed the barriers that kept them
apart. As though they had a life of their own, her
hands reached for his tie and the buttons on his shirt,
wanting to feel the furry chest that had been haunting
her for the past several days.

By the time he picked her up and laid her on his bed,
they were both bare. Stephanie seemed to have lost her
self-consciousness as she gave free rein to her need to
touch and explore him.

He felt so good to her. Her fingertips lightly caressed the muscles in his forearms and across his broad
shoulders. The swirls of dark hair on his chest captivated her. When she followed the pattern downward,
she felt his skin retract and ripple beneath her palm.

"Oh, Stephanie, love, do you have any idea what
you do to me?" He caught her earlobe gently between his teeth and tugged, then kissed her ear.

She sighed. What about what he was doing to her?
she wondered. She felt mesmerized, unable to think.
All she could do was feel what he was doing to her.
Every spot he touched on her body tingled as though
an electric current had been invisibly activated, dis-
charging tiny shock waves throughout her system.

He placed his hand lovingly around her breast, his
fingertips brushing lightly, to and fro, across her

aroused nipple. Stephanie felt as though her heart were going to leap from her chest.

Blindly, her mouth searched for his, and he obligingly met her questing lips. His tongue explored and took possession, flicking restlessly against her mouth and tongue.

No longer able to resist, he left her mouth and planted tiny little kisses down her neck until his lips encircled the rosy tip of her breast. Her restless hands clutched at his shoulders, then slid up through his hair that clung so closely to his head.

His dark hair felt like silk as it brushed against her. His hands moved urgently over her body, following the slim contours as her body narrowed at the waist, then flared gracefully at the hips. He brushed down the curve of her outer thigh, then slowly brought his hand back upward, tracing the inner shape, until it rested at the warm triangle where her thighs met.

Alex's exploration became even more intimate until Stephanie could no longer lie still. Her hands restlessly explored his muscled back, tracing the slight indentation of his spine.

He shifted until she was beneath him, pliant and eager. There was no way he could wait any longer. Carefully, he lowered himself until she had accepted him fully.

She clung to him, wanting him to extinguish the fires that he had started deep within her. When he began to move she sighed with pleasure. Yes, that was what her body was crying out for. Yes, that was the wonderful sensation she had known was waiting for her.

Yes. Oh, yes.

Their union took them beyond physical boundaries. Their minds and spirits participated in the union and commitment toward one another, becoming a communion of hearts and souls and bodies.

For a space in time they became one—whole, perfect and complete, as they each strove to bring to the other the indescribable pleasure each was experiencing. They rode the wave of ecstasy without pause, acknowledging the joy of sharing all that they were and could be, all that they possibly dreamed of being in that memorable moment.

When that wave of ecstasy reached its goal, they both let out cries of satisfaction and fulfillment, clinging to each other as though fearful they might be separated and swept away.

Alex felt exulted by Stephanie's all-encompassing participation. There could be no doubt in either one of their minds that she loved him, trusted him and that she had given herself to him without reservation.

They lay there together striving to fill their lungs with much-needed oxygen. Alex opened his eyes and gazed upon her relaxed and vulnerable expression. Her dark lashes hid her eyes from him, but not the flushed cheeks, the soft wisps of hair that clung to her forehead, or her slightly swollen lips. He smiled slightly. She definitely carried the sign of his possession.

As he watched, her lashes slowly raised until her unforgettable blue eyes stared at him. She ran her tongue across her lips, moistening them. Without hesitation he placed his mouth upon hers once more. She sighed and held him even closer.

"Oh, Alex," she managed to whisper a few moments later. Or was it hours? Who knew or cared about such unimportant items as time.

"I know, love, I know," he murmured. His mouth caressed her cheek, her nose, her forehead, her eyelids—as though he could not get enough of the taste and feel of her, as though he somehow must memorize her with his lips.

Slowly, Stephanie returned to the reality of where they were and what had just happened. The sheet was a tangle at their feet. They lay side by side, their arms and legs entwined. Alex's hand still pressed against her hips so that she was fully aligned against him, touching him from breast to thighs.

"We belong together, you know," he muttered. "Haven't we just proved that?"

"If you're expecting an argument from me, I'm afraid I can't come up with one at the moment."

He relaxed his hold so that he could pull back and appreciate the view of her lying so close to him. "We fit so well together," he pointed out and watched with amused tenderness as her entire body turned a rose hue.

"I must be out of my mind," she whispered as he leaned down and kissed her on the breast.

"Why?"

"This is unheard of. Impossibly unprofessional."

"Would you stop talking like that? For just a few hours can we forget our respective roles in life and just be Alex and Stephanie, in love, in San Francisco, with nowhere else to be for the next twelve hours except here in bed together, exploring, discovering more about each other, planning for our future? Is that so much to ask?"

His expression reminded her once again of the publicity photo she had of him. He was intently serious, his gray eyes giving nothing away. How could she have known when she first saw that picture that something like this would have happened between them? If she had known would she have been so willing to set out on the tour with him? Would she have been better prepared to face the next step in their relationship or would she have run?

Perhaps one reason that human beings are not given glimpses into their future is that they would build too many walls and barricades against the uncertainties that eventually confront them.

Since she could only live one day at a time, there was a certain amount of sense to be made that this day was the only one with which she needed to deal.

She smiled and said, "You are a marvelous lover, Colonel. I'm impressed."

He eyed her warily. She'd just made some inner shift in thinking that he hadn't followed. Her mind was so quick that he had to have the mental agility of a gymnast to keep up with her.

Life with Stephanie would never be dull, that was one truth he was ready to admit without hesitation.

"You've had so many lovers you can tell, I take it," he responded thoughtfully and watched with delight as her color turned rosy once more.

"You know better than that," she muttered.

"You're very natural, you know. And very loving. Thank you for appearing in my life. You have no idea what meeting you has done for me."

"In what way?"

"In every way. I had gotten so fixed in my way of thinking. My life has been caught up with routine for so long that I no longer had to think through my daily schedule, so much of it was habit."

"And now?"

"Now I have to work hard to keep up with you. I'm not even going to try to get ahead."

She kissed his chin, then lazily explored a path down his neck and onto his chest. "Mmm. Then you aren't going to tell me what to do?" she asked lazily as she searched for and found one of his nipples almost covered by the dark hair on his chest.

She felt his body jolt as her tongue touched the sensitive tip. She smiled to herself.

"When did you learn to do that?" he asked a little hoarsely.

Without looking up, she murmured, "Just now. From you." She quickly found the other one and gave it a similar touch.

He groaned. "Why should I tell you what to do when you have such interesting ideas of your own?" he managed to gasp.

"Then you like me to touch you?"

"Without a doubt."

"And you don't mind if I explore?"

His eyes closed. "Be my guest," he said with a sigh.

She did, until he could no longer control his need to possess her once more. The softness of her hair brushing against his sensitive skin drove him wild until finally he grabbed her around the waist and pulled her on top of him so that she straddled him.

With no hesitation she accommodated him, adjusting her body so that she slowly sheathed him until he was surrounded by her throbbing warmth. Gently, she began to move. He could feel every single motion she made in sliding over him.

Never had Alex felt so much love and attention directed toward him. She had kissed and caressed every inch of his body until he had felt as though he would explode. Now she soothed and pampered him with the promise of release, whenever he was ready.

But not now. Not just yet. He didn't want to lose this pleasurable sensation, this fantastic sharing of each other. Her eyes shone brightly in the soft light, and her mouth curved in a seductive smile that played havoc with his intentions to hang on to his restraint. Her legs were folded neatly on each side of his hips, giving her a freedom of movement that kept him continually fighting not to lose control.

Then she leaned over and kissed him, her tongue thrusting into his mouth in imitation of what they were doing, and he totally lost his hold on his concentration. He wrapped his hands around her waist as he matched her rhythm, then increased it. Faster and faster they moved together, racing toward an undetermined goal—

And then they reached it in one convulsive lunge that took both of their breaths away.

Stephanie collapsed against him as though her bones had been turned to water, which was a fairly accurate description of how Alex felt. If anyone were to yell *Fire!* at the moment, he feared he'd be unable to move to save his life.

That was his last conscious thought before sleep overtook him. Stephanie was asleep before he was.

Seven

Stephanie knew she was dreaming, but had no desire to wake up. She and Alex were lying on a beach of white sand on a secluded tropical island. He was spreading coconut oil all over her bare body. His touch felt so good to her as he smoothly stroked the oil across her breasts, down her waist and abdomen, then across her thighs.

She could feel the soft breeze as it eddied around them, the warm sun heating their bodies.

Alex stroked across her abdomen again, repeatedly sweeping over and around the area where she wanted him to touch. He would come close, teasing her with his fingers, then dart away until she shifted her hips restlessly, trying to coax him to touch her more intimately.

As though waiting for her response, his fingers moved to touch and caress her, causing a throbbing to begin. She moved her hips again, encouraging him, wanting him and then she reached to find him and discovered that he was ready for her, his smooth hardness only waiting for her invitation.

She turned to him, adjusting her body by wrapping her leg high around his hips while he moved deep inside her. Stephanie sighed with contentment and slowly opened her eyes.

She found herself looking into a smiling pair of gray eyes and a face that was flushed with passion as he moved rhythmically inside her. She clung to him, loving his touch, loving how he made her feel as he settled into a steady, pulsing rock that quickly sent her emotions reeling.

Without words, they matched each other's moves perfectly. Perhaps it was only because she had awakened from such a powerful dream that Stephanie felt she was in some magical place and time. The only part of it that was real was she and Alex—she and Alex together.

Although he had started with slow, rhythmic thrusts, their lovemaking soon escalated into breathless, heart-pounding movements that culminated in an explosion of satisfaction for both of them. When Stephanie finally managed to surface to some sense of sanity, she glanced around and noticed that the sun had risen. It was morning.

Alex continued to hold her in his arms, stroking gently down her back from neck to hips, then upward again as though soothing her. And perhaps she needed the soothing. Her body still rippled occasionally with a tremor of feeling, as though she were going through aftershocks.

"Good morning."

She couldn't believe her ears. He sounded placid and relaxed while she felt as though every muscle in her body was quivering in time to some unheard melody.

"That's quite a wake-up call you have there, Colonel. Have you ever considered having it patented?" she asked, still a little breathless.

He laughed. It was the first time she'd heard him laugh so wholeheartedly. He sounded young and very happy.

"We need to get up fairly soon if we're going to meet our schedule today," he pointed out with a grin.

His words brought Stephanie back to earth with a thump. She looked at the time. It was almost nine o'clock. They were to be at the autographing at eleven and, at the moment, her legs felt as though they had the strength of overcooked spaghetti!

"We overslept," she finally managed.

"Is that what we did?" he asked, his amusement evident in his tone. "Could have fooled me."

Pulling away from him, Stephanie sat up. And groaned.

"What's the matter, love?" he asked, suddenly serious.

She shook her head. "I'm afraid I'm not used to this type of exercise." Gingerly, she stood beside the bed, aware of muscles she never knew she had.

"I know just what you need," he said, sweeping her up in his arms and striding toward the bathroom.

"Alex! What are you doing? Put me down!"

He did—in the bathtub, while at the same time turning on the water. The hot spray hit her body and she sighed. Ah, that felt wonderful. Alex stepped in behind her and began to soap her back as she stood facing the spray.

"This feels marvelous."

His hand followed the contours of her buttocks and he replied, "It certainly does."

She glanced over her shoulder. "Colonel Sloan, sir. I had no idea of the type of man that lurked under that military bearing of yours."

He grinned. "Good. I wouldn't have wanted to give away my strategy too soon."

"What strategy?"

"You're witnessing it. Having you in my bed and shower."

She turned so that she was facing him, all the while luxuriating in the feel of the hot spray along her back. As though he never noticed her change of position, he continued to apply soap to her body, his eyes dancing.

"Alex! Stop that!"

"Stop what? I'm just saving us some time by helping you shower." Handing her the soap, he said, "Here. You can soap me if you'd like."

She discovered that there was a great deal of merit in sharing a shower with a close, intimate friend. Somehow the routine of washing a body with soap took on a whole different meaning when the body wasn't yours. She became fascinated by all the subtle, and not so subtle, differences between the body she was washing and her own.

"That's enough," he finally growled, removing her hands from him. She obligingly moved so that the spray could hit him and rinse him off while she stepped out of the shower.

Within less than a minute he had turned off the water and stepped out, grabbing a towel. He began to dry her briskly until she was forced to say, "I'm perfectly capable of drying myself, you know."

"I know. It's just all part of the wake-up service, ma'am."

She bit her lip to keep from laughing. "Whatever you say," she finally was able to get out.

Then she hurriedly let herself into her own room while he shaved and dressed. She quickly dried her hair, brushing it vigorously so that it fell in a soft cloud around her shoulders. She didn't have time to put it up this morning. And what difference did it make anyway?

With her sparkling eyes and pink cheeks, she looked more like a blushing bride than a professional publicist escorting an author on tour. And she didn't care.

Luckily the traffic was light, and they made their appointment with time to spare. Once again Stephanie took her place in the background and waited for the time to pass. She amused herself by watching how Alex responded to people, then reminded herself of how he had responded to her earlier that morning.

As he smiled and joked, she mentally caressed his broad shoulders and arms, ran her fingers through his closely cropped hair and nibbled on his earlobe. At one point he jerked his head up and looked over at her as though the intensity of her thoughts had reached him. She nodded solemnly at him, and for a moment he looked confused. Then someone called his name and he turned away from her.

By the time they got away from the crowd and crawled into the taxi that was taking them back to their hotel, Alex was pulling off his tie and pushing it into his coat pocket. "I'm ready to get out of these clothes and into something more casual. This has been quite a week, one way or the other."

His grin made it clear that he was thinking of more than the tour, and when Stephanie dropped her gaze, he laughed out loud.

When they arrived at the hotel, Alex paid the cabbie, took her arm, and they crossed the immense lobby of the luxury hotel toward the elevators.

"First, let's get into something more comfortable," he murmured in her ear. "What do you suggest, your bed or mine?"

Stephanie laughed, knowing her face was flushed, not only by his suggestion but by her earlier fantasies of the morning. "Really, Alex, I can't believe that—"

"Stephanie?"

Coming to an abrupt stop, Stephanie watched as a well-dressed businessman made his way across the lobby to her. Kent. Kent was here. She glanced at her watch. It was a few minutes past two o'clock.

Trying to get a grip on her composure, she forced herself to smile and say, "Oh, hi, Kent. Sorry I'm late. The autographing ran over."

She saw the look of shocked surprise in his face and couldn't really blame him for his reaction. She knew what she and Alex must look like. His arm had been around her waist, his hand resting intimately on her hip. She'd been laughing up at him, obviously responding to what he'd been saying. They must have looked like just what they were—two lovers hastening back to the privacy of their room.

Stephanie had completely forgotten about Kent and his phone call two days ago. It was as though he had ceased to exist, this man who only a few weeks ago she'd planned to marry!

She shook her head, trying to clear it. "Kent, I'd like you to meet Colonel Alexander Sloan. Alex, this is Kent Caulder, a friend of mine from New York."

Alex had dropped his arm from around her when Kent had joined them, but he still stood close beside her. He held out his hand to the younger man and said, "How do you do, Mr. Caulder."

Kent's eyes had never left Stephanie, not since she had described him as a friend. Slowly, his gaze ran over her flushed face and windswept hair, then he looked at Alex. Reluctantly, he took the hand that was being offered to him.

"Colonel," he said, with only the barest of acknowledgements. Then turning his gaze back to Stephanie, he asked, "Are you ready to go?"

Stephanie felt like a fool. How could she have forgotten Kent? She glanced apologetically at Alex whose expression gave no hint as to his thoughts. "If you'll excuse me, Alex. I made an appointment with Kent earlier and—"

"Yes, I know," he said quietly. "I'll see you later." Nodding to Kent he said, "Nice meeting you," and continued toward the elevators without a backward glance.

Stephanie watched him go and felt a keen desire to rush after him and try to explain, but she wasn't sure what she needed to say. She felt deserted, somehow, and yet she was the one who had made the plans, not Alex.

"Have you had lunch?" Kent asked quietly.

She shook her head. "No."

"Then I know the perfect place." He held out his hand and smiled. "Come on. I'll show you."

That's when she remembered. This was Kent, whom she had known for years and loved like a brother. And he wanted to talk to her about something. Maybe it wouldn't take very long and she could get back to Alex and to—

Stephanie couldn't allow her thoughts to go any further. She had to concentrate on Kent and what he was saying.

Kent began to ask casual questions about the tour and how it was going. Her replies were brief, but she couldn't help it. She wasn't in the mood for casual conversation.

After they arrived at the restaurant and ordered, she interrupted his telling her about something to do with his business by saying, "Why did you want to see me, Kent? What's so important that it couldn't have waited another week or so until we were both back in New York?"

Kent sighed and leaned toward her slightly. "I missed you, Stephanie."

"I don't know what you mean, Kent. We've gone weeks where we didn't see each other. We both understand how hectic our schedules are. What's different now?"

He held up her left hand and indicated her bare ring finger. "This is what's different. We always knew where we stood with each other before."

"We know where we stand now, Kent. You made that clear a few weeks ago."

"That's partly what I want to talk to you about."

"You mean Susan wasn't as exciting as you thought once the engagement was broken?"

"Don't, Stephanie. Please. That doesn't even sound like you. I know I hurt you. I was hurting, too, and confused. I needed some time to think, to evaluate all that had happened. Neither one of us have ever allowed our emotions to take control and make decisions for us. I'll admit I was rattled." He met her steady gaze with one of his own. "I love you, Steph. I hate what's happened between us. I want you back in my life."

She sighed. "Kent, whether you like it or not, there's no way we can go back to where we were. What happened can't just be made to disappear. We can't pretend that everything's the same between us. I appreciated the fact that you were honest with me. I still do."

"I'm trying to be just as honest now. It took me a while to realize that I was flattered by Susan's confession and her interest in me as a man, rather than just a business associate. But I also came to the realization that the only thing about me that was truly touched was my ego." He slowly tapped his finger on the rim of his water glass, watching as the ice tinkled in clear tones against the crystal.

When he glanced back at her, she saw real anguish in his eyes. "I want to marry you, Steph, more than I've ever wanted anything in my life. Maybe it was better that this came up now and I got it out of my system before the wedding. I don't want to lose you." He reached into the inside pocket of his suit and pulled out her engagement ring. "Will you take this back?"

She stared at the ring as though it were a snake ready to strike. Slowly, she began to shake her head.

"No," was all she could find to say.

Kent placed the ring on the table between them. "No? Just like that? With no explanation? No reasons at all?"

Stephanie tried to marshal her thoughts, tried to find a way to explain to him what she had yet to attempt to put into words for herself.

Finally, she spoke. "Kent, your instincts were more right about us than you knew at the time. You were one hundred percent correct. What we have between us is a loving relationship, a mutual support, a basic respect and caring that I'll always treasure."

His face began to brighten at her words, and she forced herself to go on.

"But it isn't enough for a marriage."

"How can you possibly know that?"

"I just do. One of the reasons I love you is because I'm so comfortable with you. On this trip I recognized why. I love you in the same way I love my brothers. I'm interested in you and what happens to you, but I've never had the sense that I couldn't live without you in my life."

"And you have that sense about someone now, don't you?"

Why did he have to be so perceptive? she wondered, knowing that he knew her too well not to have read the signs earlier.

"Yes," she acknowledged with a slight nod.

"And how does he feel about it?"

"I believe the same way."

"This happened rather fast, didn't it?"

Again she nodded. "Yes. Yes, it did."

"Is it possible that you could be mistaken?"

"There's always that possibility. But I really don't think so. And time is the only real way to measure my feelings."

He took her hand and squeezed it. "If it's all right with you, I'd like to give what we share time, then. I don't want to walk out of your life. You've just described how I feel about you, and I've already tested it with time."

"Oh, Kent," she murmured, almost feeling his pain. "I'm sorry."

"Yes, I believe you. And so am I. I've been trying to put everything that's happened in the past where it belongs, but you don't know what I'd give to be able to go back and undo our break-up."

When their meal arrived, they both looked at their food as though wondering why they'd ordered it. Forcing herself to pick up her fork, Stephanie glanced up and asked, "Now tell me about this latest presentation you were describing earlier."

They both knew the personal discussion was over. So was a part of the life they had shared together.

After their meal, Kent and Stephanie found a park where they could walk and enjoy the spring day. They fell into easy conversation, the same type of companionable discussions that had first drawn them together years ago. Their mutual respect was still intact.

After more than an hour of walking, Stephanie pointed to a park bench. "I needed the exercise, I'll admit, but my legs are already complaining." What she didn't want to admit was how little sleep she had gotten the night before or why. She concentrated her attention and energy on the present. Stephanie couldn't allow her thoughts to wander back to Alex, wondering what he was doing and how long it would be before she could suggest to Kent that she needed to return to the hotel.

She should have known that Kent would have noticed her silence. "You're in love with the colonel, aren't you?" he said into the silence, effectively drawing her thoughts back to him.

"What makes you ask that?"

"Because I saw you when you walked into the hotel with him. I've known you for a long time, Steph, and I've never seen you that way before. You looked alive...radiant...as though your very skin glowed." He touched a wave of hair that rested on her shoulder. "Even your hair seems filled with energy. You don't wear it down that way very often."

"That's true," she said, not wanting to get into any explanations regarding why it was down today.

"It happened fast, didn't it?"

She looked at Kent and saw that he really wanted to know. She reminded herself that they were friends first, had been friends for a long time.

Stephanie nodded. "Yes. It happened very quickly."

"What about him? How does he feel?"

She gazed off into the distance. "I'm not really sure at this point." Glancing back at Kent, she smiled wryly. "I'm not very good at figuring out what men think and feel. Who knows? Maybe it's because we've been together so much. Perhaps once we get back to our regular routines we'll both look at the relationship differently."

"But you don't think you'll feel any differently, do you?"

"No. I think what has happened to me would have happened no matter how we met or how long we were around each other."

"Oh, Steph. I don't want you to get hurt."

"If it happens, it happens."

"Just don't forget that I'm going to always be there if you need me."

She touched his hand that rested on his thigh. "Thank you. I appreciate that."

He glanced at his watch. "What would you like to do this evening?"

"I promised Alex I'd have dinner with him tonight. I made the arrangement before I talked with you."

He stood and pulled her up beside him. "I understand. I really appreciate your spending the afternoon with me."

She tucked her arm under his, and they began walking toward the entrance to the park. "I've enjoyed seeing you again, too, Kent. I have really missed what we shared. Even when we talked on the phone before I left, there was something not right about us."

"My guilty conscience, for one thing. And my embarrassment. I didn't know what to say, even then. I had sat there like a fool and allowed you to return the ring, knowing in my heart that it was the worst thing that could happen, but feeling paralyzed to stop what was playing out between us." They reached his rental car and he unlocked it, helping her inside.

Once he was behind the wheel and driving, Stephanie said, "It was the best thing that could have happened, Kent—for both of us. I think that during our relationship we were both too caught up in what we were thinking, rather than what we were feeling. We've both had a chance to get in touch with those feelings. That was important."

"But even after getting in touch with them, I realized that you were what I wanted in life."

She touched his shoulder lightly. "Maybe. Maybe not. Perhaps you wanted to return to what was safe and secure in your life. We did provide that sort of stable base for each other while we were getting our careers off the ground. Maybe it's time that we branch out and get involved in something new."

They stopped in front of the hotel and he got out. "Who knows? Maybe you're right. At the moment all I can think about is what I've lost."

They crossed the lobby and got into the elevator. When they reached her floor, he walked her down the hallway before she said, "You haven't lost anything, Kent. I'm still here. I'll always be here whenever you need me."

He took both of her hands in his and smiled. "Thank you for that, love. Thank you for being so warm and caring...and so understanding. No wonder I love you."

"I love you, too, Kent."

She slipped her arms around his shoulders and kissed him in the same way she would kiss any one of her brothers. He hugged her to him for a moment, then reluctantly stepped away. "Take care of yourself. Call me when you get back to New York."

"I will. Have a good meeting tomorrow."

"I'll do my best." With a brief wave Kent turned and went back to the elevators.

Stephanie let herself into her room. It seemed strange to her, unlived in. The bed was still turned back from the night before because she had never slept in it.

Going to the connecting door, she tapped lightly and waited, but there was no answer. She hadn't asked Alex his plans that afternoon. Since she had forgotten about her meeting with Kent, she had assumed that she and Alex would spend the time together.

She had a hunch he'd thought the same thing.

Now that she was alone, Stephanie experienced a letdown, as though all of her energy had deserted her. She decided to lie down for a while and rest. After slipping off her outer clothes and her shoes, she crawled beneath the covers and stretched out with a sigh.

She had a great deal to think about, but nothing that couldn't wait for a few hours. Stephanie drifted off to sleep, her thoughts on Alex and what sort of future she might have with him.

When she opened her eyes some time later, the room was in deep shadows. She lay there for a moment trying to wake up. Her sleepy gaze took in her limited view of the bedside table, the larger, round table in front of the window and the chair sitting by it.

Alex sat there, gazing pensively out the window.

She studied his profile, content to watch him unobserved for a moment. There was so much strength in his face. She mentally traced the shape of his nose, his mouth and his firm chin. She loved the way his military-style haircut faithfully outlined the regal shape of his head.

Seeing him made her want to touch him, and she stirred. He reacted to the slight sound by turning his head and looking at her.

"Hello," she said in a sleep-drugged voice.

His mouth lifted in a half smile. "Hello, yourself."

"Have you been waiting long? You should have awakened me."

"I was tempted to, believe me, but I reminded myself that you needed your rest. I hope you don't mind my waiting in here for you."

She sat up and stretched, then pushed the covers away and stood. "I'm glad you did." She still wore her slip, and felt unself-conscious as she went over to him and sank down into his lap. "I missed you today," she said, offering him a kiss.

His arms came around her tightly, and he returned her kiss with feverish intensity. Stephanie felt as though she were melting in his embrace—her arms and legs seemed to have lost all consistency. Would his kiss always affect her that way?

When he finally lifted his head, she sighed and contentedly rested her head on his shoulder.

"Are you hungry?" he asked. She smiled. She could feel the vibration of his voice in his chest. His words rumbled beneath her ear.

"A little."

"I did some exploring this afternoon. Found what looked to be a great restaurant, so I made reservations for us."

"How much time do we have?"

"A couple of hours. There's no hurry."

"Good," she said with another soft sigh, snuggling closer to his chin.

"Stephanie?"

"Hmm?"

"Kent is the man you were engaged to, isn't he?"

She could feel herself tensing, despite everything she could do to prevent a reaction. Without raising her head she finally said, "Yes."

"Why are you no longer engaged?"

She thought about that for a few moments. He didn't rush her, but continued to hold her close, softly stroking her hair and her back in a comforting rhythm.

"We misjudged friendship for something more," she explained after several minutes of silence.

"He's still in love with you."

"I love him, too, but not in the way he needs. I value his friendship."

"I saw the look on his face when he saw us together earlier. He knows we're lovers, doesn't he?"

"He didn't ask and I didn't tell him. I didn't consider it to be any of his business."

He pulled her closer, his hand lingering across the flowing line of her hip and thigh as she lay curled up in the chair with him. "I want more from you than friendship, Steph. I love you. I want everything you have to give. I could never be so gracious as to smile and walk away from you. I think you should know that."

She raised her head. "I'm not a possession, Alex."

"I know. But it scares me, what I feel for you. Having you in my life has made me look at everything so differently. And I'm not sure what I would do if I didn't know that you were there—somewhere—for me."

"I'm here, Alex. I'm right here, right now. This is all that anyone is given, don't you see? It's this precious present—the now—this is the only thing any of us has."

He picked her up and stood there, holding her in his arms. "I want to make love to you. I want to show you what you make me feel whenever I'm with you. Let me show you," he whispered, brushing his lips against hers.

She nodded, unable to speak. He set her on her feet and quickly removed the remaining items of clothing, then gently eased her onto the bed. With a speed that would have been appropriate for an air drill, Alex disrobed and sat down beside her, enjoying the look of her, the feel of her, the delicate scent of her. With slow movements, he leaned over and lightly touched his tongue to the very tip of her breast. He felt her quiver beneath him. Yes, he especially enjoyed the taste of her.

Stephanie lay waiting, discovering the added sense of anticipation in watching him as he sat there silently exploring her with his eyes. Her pulse began to race at the look of desire in his eyes, and when his fingertips brushed lightly against her breasts, her breath caught in her throat.

With a delicacy of touch, Alex began to worship her with his hands, his mouth and his tongue—touching her, caressing her, taking possession of her inch by inch as he began at her head and worked down to the tips of her toes. He never missed a spot.

With each touch Stephanie's skin sprang to life, tingling with expectancy and awareness. He kissed each area, nuzzling affectionately until she could not lie still. She reached for him but he captured her hands with one of his.

"This is all for you, love."

"But I want to hold you," she whimpered, shifting restlessly under his probing, teasing touch.

"Later... not now. I wouldn't be able to concentrate if you touched me at the moment."

"I can't concentrate *now*," she managed to reply in a gasp.

He smiled. "Good. Just lie back and enjoy it."

Enjoy it! He was driving her crazy. She couldn't lie still. Her body felt as though she'd been hooked up to receive some persistent electric charge, and with each touch the tingle intensified.

"Alex!" she finally cried. Her body had taken over. She was mindlessly responding to him as he continued to use his tongue and fingers to produce the most incredible sensations within her. She felt totally seduced by his titillating explorations.

Stephanie had never experienced anything like this before. How could one man be able to produce such reactions in her, cause her to lose such complete control of herself that she was begging him to give her some release from the shivering, trembling sensations he was evoking?

By the time he moved over her and lowered himself into her arms, she was almost crying with need for him. When he filled her, she drew her legs tightly around him as though refusing to ever let him go.

"It's all right, love," he whispered, kissing her on her cheeks, the tip of her nose, her forehead, "I'm here now. I'm here."

Stephanie was almost sobbing with relief. He felt so good and she needed him so much.

He continued to control their lovemaking, moving in long, slow strokes while he gave her all-consuming kisses. This was what she had wanted. She knew that now. This marvelous sense of oneness, of unity, of total and complete sharing.

Now it was hers. Now it was theirs. This was something they had created together, and it was good.

Alex prolonged their lovemaking as much as he physically could, but he, too, was a prisoner of the sensations he had created for both of them.

By the time he reached his peak, she had experienced multiple releases. She clung to him as he cried out his fulfillment and satiation and collapsed beside her on the bed.

When he finally stirred she was almost asleep again, content to lay entwined with him. Alex lifted his head and looked at her. "Are you all right?"

She smiled. She knew her expression was smug, but she couldn't help it. There was no way anyone could possibly remove that smile from her face. "All right is an understatement at the moment."

"We need to get ready if we're going to keep our reservations."

"Okay," she said, without moving.

"Would you rather not go out?"

"And miss a chance to have dinner with you in San Francisco? Surely, you jest."

Reluctantly, Alex began to unwind from around her. "Then let's get up," he said, lifting her from the bed and onto her feet.

She looked up at him and grinned. "You mean you aren't going to carry me?"

He began to laugh. "I've got all I can handle at the moment to carry myself. I don't know what I thought I was proving just now."

She slid her arms around his waist and hugged him. "Whatever it was, I'm convinced."

They wandered into the bathroom and took turns standing under the hot spray of water, lovingly soaping each other. Stephanie felt as though she had always showered this way and couldn't imagine how she could not have known the joy of bathing her lover.

By the time they got out, they were both aroused once again but determined to ignore it. Amid a rumbling of forgotten stomachs a sense of hilarity had taken over, and they were laughing and teasing each other while they dried off.

They were dressed in short order, downstairs and climbing into a cab by the time they could look at each other without bursting into laughter.

Stephanie had discovered another hitherto unknown facet of Alex's personality—he had a wicked sense of humor and he was fun to be with. How had he so successfully hidden that playful part of himself behind his stern military exterior?

Dinner at Fisherman's Wharf was everything Stephanie could have wished for. The food was superbly cooked and the view of the bay through the wide plate-glass windows, breathtaking. They sat and watched the sailboats return to shore as the light faded.

Stephanie gazed at the brightly burning candle on their table and smiled. Candlelight seemed to have a magical quality about it as it flickered in unseen currents of air. The fresh flowers had a more intense scent as well, or was it just her own senses that seemed to have been opened up and expanded to include everything around her?

She looked over at Alex and saw that he was watching her with a very warm expression on his face.

Impulsively, she reached over and touched his hand as it rested around the stem of his wineglass. "Thank you for bringing me. This really is lovely."

"I hoped you would enjoy it."

"I do. Very much."

"Good, then I've set the right mood to ask you to marry me, haven't I?"

His tone was light and teasing, but his eyes held a shadow of vulnerability that deeply touched her.

"Are you sure?"

He took her hand. "More sure than I've ever been about anything in my whole life. I want to spend the rest of my life with you."

"I love you, Alex. There's no question about that. But things are so complicated. You live in Washington. My job is in New York. We're both so busy..."

"We can work all of that out once we decide what we want."

"I want you to be happy. I'm not sure I know how to do that."

"By being who you are. By loving me. That's all that matters. We can work out everything else. Will you accept and believe that?"

Slowly she nodded her head. Right now she would believe and accept anything. Somehow they would work everything out. It might take some time, but they had all the rest of their lives.

"Yes, Alex. I'll marry you."

"When?"

She began to laugh. "Don't you think we need to take some time to get better acquainted? I want you to meet my family." She shook her head, suddenly remembering her brother. "Oh, boy. Dave's never going to believe there wasn't something between us in Denver."

"Dave's a very perceptive man. I'm sure he could sense all the undercurrents between us even then."

"Well, let me warn you, Colonel Sloan, that when I tell my family that we're engaged, you're going to be put through an interrogation that will make any military procedure seem mild."

"Did Kent go through a similar processing?"

"Not really, no. Most of the family had met him when they visited me in New York. They knew we were friends. No one was particularly surprised when I accepted his ring."

"Will you accept my ring?"

She nodded. "Whenever you wish to give it to me."

He sighed with relief. "Good. I was afraid you were going to give me trouble about the fact that you had recently broken an engagement, that you needed more time."

"Now I can't tell whether you're relieved I didn't mention it or disappointed that I didn't put up more of a struggle."

His bright grin flashed across his face. "To be honest, I'd marshaled all sorts of arguments to combat any opposition you could have given me. Just look at all the energy we're saving by not going into all that."

"Alex, one of the things you no doubt have learned about me is that I generally understand my own mind and what I want, even though there are times when I don't always know how to get it." She paused, thinking. "As in this case. I would love to tell you that I'll rush right back to New York and hand in my resignation so that I can join you in Washington, but I can't do that. I've worked hard to get to where I am. I can't just turn my back on it."

"I understand that. Remember, I've worked with you. I know how seriously you take what you do." He squeezed her hand. "We'll figure something out. Just give it a chance, all right?"

She nodded. "All right."

And later, when they were curled up together in Alex's bed after spending time loving each other, Stephanie felt that everything would work out for them if only she believed it would.

However, when the phone rang in the middle of the night, reality intruded on their magical time together, effectively destroying all their fantasies and plans.

Eight

When the phone first rang, Stephanie thought it was the alarm and she reached groggily toward the side of the bed before she realized it was only a little after midnight.

Then she heard Alex's voice, sounding amazingly awake.

"Alex Sloan."

She was lying on his arm and she shifted so that he could move if he needed to.

"What's up?" he asked, his voice sounding sharp and intense.

Stephanie began to feel uneasy. A call this late at night was generally an emergency. She wondered what was wrong.

There was no way to tell from Alex's conversation. His questions were brief. Whoever was on the other end of the line was doing a considerable amount of talking.

Finally, Alex said, "All right. I should be there within an hour." Something was said at the other end and he added, "I understand. Yes. I'll get right on it."

He was out of bed by the time he'd put the phone down, reaching for his clothes.

"Alex! Who was that? What's wrong? Where are you going?"

"I've got to leave. I'm sorry. Something's come up."

"What do you mean, leave? You can't leave. We're flying to Los Angeles, then on to Dallas and Atlanta. You can't just walk out now."

He'd already dressed while she was protesting. He was now pulling on his socks and shoes, then walking into the bathroom. "It can't be helped. You'll have to postpone the tour or something. I have to leave."

She grabbed up the spread and wrapped it around her bare body, then followed him into the bathroom. He'd already plugged in his electric shaver and was rapidly going over his jawline.

"But where are you going?"

"I'm not at liberty to say. This is part of my job, Stephanie." His eyes met hers in the mirror and she saw the regret in them. "I'm sorry I can't tell you more."

"You're sorry! Is that all you can say? We're in the middle of a very important tour, trying to publicize your book. Don't you care?"

He unplugged his razor and turned toward her. "Of course I care. If I can get back to you before it's over, I will."

"Get back to me! Don't you understand? I can't do this without you. You're the one everyone wants to meet, to hear speak. I'll have to cancel everything!"

"Maybe we can do it some other time," he said, stepping past her and rapidly throwing his things into his suitcase.

"This doesn't make any sense," she said, shaking her head in confusion. "I must be dreaming. I'll wake up in the morning and we'll both laugh about it."

He picked up his bag and started toward her. He paused as though trying to think of something to say. "I'll call you as soon as I can," he finally said. Then he kissed her, a hard, brief kiss that revealed more than any words that his mind was already onto other things.

"Where? Where will you call me?"

He opened the door and glanced back. "I'm not sure. New York, probably."

"You're really leaving, then. You're just walking out on the tour, with no explanation—nothing."

He frowned. "I don't have time to discuss it. There should be a car waiting for me downstairs right at this moment. I'll be in touch."

And with those words, he was gone.

Stephanie stood there in the middle of his room, feeling like a statue. Gradually she looked around. There was the bed where they had slept. The covers were tossed back. There was nothing else in the room that indicated Alexander Sloan had ever been there.

Nothing but her memories of him.

He was gone. He had left her to deal with the chore of contacting everyone along the remainder of the tour and trying to explain that something important had come up that had precedence for him.

He hadn't even tried to argue or explain. It was as though whoever had called owned him, body and soul, and nothing else, nobody else, really mattered.

Stephanie was forced to face the fact that she didn't know this man. Not at all. All she knew was that when he left he had taken her heart with him.

She let herself into her own room. Feeling chilled, she found her nightgown and slipped it on, then got under the covers and lay there. There was so much for her to do, so many people to call, cancellations to be made.

There was no reason for her to catch the flight to L.A. in a few hours. She would call the airline and cancel the flight and see about returning to New York.

But not now. It was too early. She had to get through the next few hours. She needed to sleep, if she could. Stephanie felt as though she'd been floating in a wonderful pink bubble, protected from the world. Now her bubble had burst and she was dumped back into reality.

The man she thought she knew would never have walked out on her this way. He was too considerate, too understanding, too gentle to create so many problems.

What had she done? Created the man in her mind that she wanted Colonel Alexander Sloan to be? Who was he? What was he? And why did she have such a deep, aching pain inside, clawing to surface, to inundate her with so much hurt?

Stephanie knew what she had to do to terminate the tour. She wasn't sure what she was going to do to get over this pain.

By midafternoon, Stephanie boarded a flight to New York. She had spent the morning on the telephone—explaining, apologizing, soothing and consoling. Right now she had a headache that was the granddaddy of all headaches. Hopefully she could sleep most of the way.

Stephanie managed to doze until the flight attendant checked with her to see what she wanted to eat. She knew she had to eat something, and without much interest she made her choice. Glancing at the man seated beside her, she did a double take. He was reading Alex's novel.

Was she ever going to be able to get away from the reminders? She had called Harry Mattingly to report that she was coming home early. He'd been concerned that the tour was cut short, but pleased with the result of added book sales in the cities where they had visited. Obviously, the publisher would be pleased with the numbers that proved the tour to be a wise venture.

At least the tour had been wise for everyone professionally. Stephanie wondered how long it would take her to recover.

The real problem, she was discovering, was that she missed Alex. They had been together almost constantly for a week. She should have been thoroughly sick of the man by that time and eager to be returning home. Instead, all she could think about was how he had looked signing books, how well his jacket had fit across his shoulders as he stood before a listening audience and talked to them.

Whenever she pictured him in bed with her, Stephanie would squirm and force herself to focus on another subject. She tried to look at the situation more objectively. Hadn't Laura suggested that she have a fling to forget Kent? That was almost amusing. Too bad she didn't feel much like laughing.

Stephanie had known better. She knew not to get involved. Traveling the way they had been was too artificial. There was nothing realistic about it. They had turned to each other as buddies, in a grueling schedule that took everything they had just to continue.

So they had found each other attractive. What was wrong with that? Alex had said all the right things. He'd made her feel loved and cherished. He'd proposed marriage. Hadn't that meant something?

What? If he had been sincere, could he have actually jumped out of bed with her to go rushing away in the middle of the night without an explanation?

The trouble was that Stephanie had no idea. She didn't know what to think . . . about anything. All she knew was that when she got home she wanted to get into bed and stay there for a week. At least.

It was almost midnight when she got to her apartment. She unlocked the door and discovered that Laura had the night chain on.

"Laura? Hey, let me in, will you?"

She could see Laura's light come on, and she watched through the slit in the door as her roommate came out of her room.

"Steph? Is that you?"

"Yes." She pulled the door closed while Laura fumbled with the chain. The door was flung open. She picked up her bag and stepped inside.

"What are you doing here?" Laura demanded.

"I happen to live here, Laura."

"You know I don't mean that. You're supposed to be in L.A." She scratched her head. "Or is it Dallas? I forget."

"Frankly, so do I. It doesn't matter, anyway. The remainder of the tour was canceled."

"Canceled! What do you mean, canceled? You worked for weeks getting that thing set up. What happened?"

"Colonel Sloan happened. He couldn't stick around long enough to finish the schedule." Stephanie carried her bag into her room and placed it on the cedar chest that sat at the end of her bed.

Everything looked so familiar. This was her real life. Not passionate lovemaking in a luxury hotel, not dining by candlelight, overlooking the San Francisco Bay. She just needed to keep her perspective.

"I can't believe the man!" Laura was saying, following Stephanie into her room. "After all you've done. What was his excuse for calling off the tour?"

"He didn't bother to give one. He just left."

"Did you two have words? If so, I'm not surprised. He sounds like a most irritating man."

"Do you suppose we could postpone this discussion until morning? I'm beat. It's been a rather harrowing day."

Laura walked over to Stephanie and hugged her. "I'm sure it has. Can I get you something to drink, maybe some hot chocolate or something to relax?"

Stephanie shook her head. "No. I just want to get into bed. I haven't gotten much sleep lately." Her mind cringed away from the thought.

"Sure. Are you going into the office tomorrow?"

"I don't think so. Harry knows what happened. He said to come in whenever I was ready to return to work." Glancing toward her suitcase, she shook her head and said, "He doesn't know what he may be inviting."

Laura patted her arm. "You're just tired, Steph. Get some sleep. I'll talk to you when I get home tomorrow." She smiled and went into her room.

Stephanie took a shower, hoping it would relax her. Instead, all she could think about was the showers she had shared with Alex. *Stop it!* she told herself. Just because she wasn't the type of person to indulge in casual affairs, she had to come to terms with the fact that she had done that very thing. It wouldn't kill her. As a matter of fact, it merely confirmed what she had always known to be true: she wasn't cut out for that sort of thing. She got too involved, felt too much and hurt too much when the affair was over.

Curling up later with her extra pillow in her arms, Stephanie forced herself to relax, concentrated on blanking out her thoughts and eventually fell asleep... only to dream about Alex.

"Good morning, Harry," she said two days later. "I'm back."

He looked up from the papers on his desk. "Good. How do you feel?"

"Like a new woman. I'm ready to get to work."

"Glad to hear it. How would you like to take a couple of romance writers and an editor to Hawaii for a big promotion they want to have over there?"

She sat up. "Are you serious?"

"Yep. Got the call yesterday. They want to schedule it for September."

She picked up her pad and pen. "What are the details?" Within minutes Stephanie was concentrating on work, pleased to have something to keep her busy.

The weeks passed slowly, but they passed. At first, every time the phone would ring, Stephanie's heart would leap to her throat. But it was never Alex. Why had she ever thought it would be?

As time went on, she finally accepted how easily she had been taken in. He was a virile, handsome and charismatic man who had worked his charms on the most available female. Why hadn't she seen that before? Of course she felt like a fool for believing him. But she wasn't the first woman to have fallen for sincere good looks and hungry eyes, and she knew she wouldn't be the last.

Stephanie was getting better at pushing all thoughts of Alex away as soon as they appeared. Unfortunately, she wasn't as successful in dealing with her dreams. More than once she had awakened to find that she'd been crying in her sleep, just like some silly schoolgirl.

She turned thirty in July, and Kent took her out on the town to celebrate. He'd never mentioned Alex to her. Not once. She would always love him for that, if for nothing else. He also never mentioned the possibility of their getting married. He knew she wasn't seeing anyone else and seemed to find that encouraging.

Without realizing it, Stephanie slowly slipped back into the pattern of her life before she'd met Alex. She lunched with friends, went to an occasional Broadway show in a group that usually included Laura, and saw Kent whenever he was in town.

So why wasn't she happy? What had changed? Her job was just as fulfilling, her friendships were just as valuable. She had everything she could possibly want, didn't she?

There were never any unexpected phone calls.

The day after Labor Day was hot, and Stephanie was already counting the days until she left for Hawaii. Thank God Harry had assigned this trip to her. There were only three days of actual appearances involved, but she had decided to take another week's vacation and stay in Hawaii on her own.

She needed the time off. She'd been driving herself all summer, either with work or a busy social calendar. It was time to relax and to come to terms with her feelings about life and what she wanted from it.

When her secretary buzzed her on the intercom, Stephanie didn't look up. "Yes?" she asked, still writing.

"There's someone here to see you."

Since very few people came to the office without an appointment, Stephanie glanced up in surprise and saw a very familiar pair of gray eyes staring at her through the glass partition that separated her office from her secretary's.

Stephanie pushed her chair back and slowly stood, maintaining eye contact with the man she never had expected to see again.

He was in uniform, the first time she'd ever seen him like that, and he looked devastating. The air-force blue enhanced his dark tan and hair. Her eyes seemed to devour him as he stood there waiting for her to walk around her desk and come to the door.

He looked thinner. There were deep lines around his mouth that hadn't been there last spring. But his tall, lean figure was shown to good advantage by his military stance, his shoulders looking as broad as ever.

"Colonel Sloan?" she said, pleased that her voice sounded businesslike and aloof. "What a surprise. Won't you come in?"

He nodded and walked past her. She glanced at her secretary and saw the woman's mouth slightly ajar. Yes, the man definitely had what could be described as sex appeal. She only hoped she had been immunized against the symptoms that seemed to have overtaken her hapless secretary.

"Won't you sit down?" she asked, indicating one of the chairs pulled up in front of her desk. Without looking at him again, she walked back around her desk to her chair and sat down. Picking up her pen, she bounced it lightly against the pad she'd been writing on. "What brings you to New York, Colonel?"

Alex slowly settled back into his chair and studied the woman across from him. He had known that this meeting wasn't going to be easy. He had known that he owed her a great many explanations—which he had planned with great care—but seeing the cool, professional woman across from him forced him to reevaluate some of his thinking.

He'd always worked under the assumption that she would want to hear his explanations, would in fact demand them. He had anticipated her anger or possible resentment. What he hadn't expected was indifference.

Seated across from him was the woman he'd first seen at the Philadelphia airport, only less friendly, if that was possible. Her hair was pulled high off her neck, and her dress looked cool but elegant. This was her environment, and she looked comfortable. Her expression was guarded but calm as she waited for him to speak.

Several times during the past two weeks he had picked up the phone to call her. Each time he'd replaced the instrument without ever completing the series of numbers that would have connected them. He'd known that he had to see her. He'd wanted to be with her, to hold her, to reassure her.

Now he wondered why he'd bothered to come. However, she had asked what he was doing there. He needed to say something.

"I'm here on business," he said as noncommittally as possible.

"I see. How's your book coming?" she asked in a polite tone of voice.

So, she thought he was here because of his writing. Perhaps it was just as well. Did he really want to make a complete fool of himself, now that he understood just how little the time they had spent together on the West Coast meant to her?

"I'm afraid I haven't had much time for it lately," he explained quietly.

"I notice that *Bridges to Burn* made the *New York Times* bestseller list. I know you must be pleased," she offered, wondering why he wasn't saying more. What was he doing here? What did he want? She glanced down and saw that her hand holding the pen was trembling. She unobtrusively released the pen and placed her hand in her lap.

He cleared his throat. "Actually, that was one of the reasons I stopped by to see you. I had hoped that perhaps you'd let me take you to dinner tonight. It was through your efforts that the book has done so well."

She shook her head. "The book has done well because it was a very good book. No amount of promotion can make a book sell if it isn't a readable, compelling story."

Alex leaned forward slightly and said, "Does that mean you won't have dinner with me tonight?"

Stephanie could feel the hated color flood her cheeks. What could she say? Should she tell him she was busy? After all, this was very short notice. Did she want to spend any more time with this man? Hadn't she been in enough pain without exposing herself to additional hurt?

He obviously wanted to see her again, but why? What did he want? Did he really expect that she would fall into his arms again after months of silence between them? She could read nothing from his expression, but then, he'd always been good at masking what he was thinking or feeling. *Most of the time,* she reminded herself. *Then there were other times....*

"Uh, no. That's not what I meant at all. I'd like to have dinner with you, Alex. Thank you." *Of course you would, you ninny, because you're a masochist at heart. You enjoy probing at wounds to see how well they have healed, don't you?*

His sudden smile caught her off guard. It was the first time he'd smiled since she'd seen him that morning. He actually appeared relieved, as though he'd been afraid she would turn him down.

Alex stood and said, "I won't take up any more of your time then. If you'll give me your home address, I'll pick you up at seven."

"Or I could meet you somewhere," she offered.

"No," he stated firmly. "I'll pick you up."

She shrugged. If he wanted to chase all over Manhattan to pick her up, that was fine with her. She had just been trying to save him some inconvenience. After writing down her apartment address and phone number, she stood and handed him the slip of paper.

"Thank you," he said, glancing briefly at the paper. He turned to leave, then looked at her appraisingly. "I'll see you later."

"That will be fine, Colonel," she offered as he walked out of the room.

What am I doing? she wondered as her gaze followed him until he was out of sight. *I must be crazy.* But she was going to see him again. One more time would help to tie off the remnants of their association. In May their separation had been too abrupt, too brutal, leaving so many unanswered questions. Perhaps now she would be able to deal with what had happened between them and release it, putting it in its proper place in her past.

"You're going to dinner with whom?" Laura demanded shortly after Stephanie arrived home.

"You heard me." Stephanie was already in the bathroom, turning on the shower.

"Oh, I heard you. I just wondered if what I heard was what you said. I could have sworn you said Alex Sloan."

Stephanie stepped into the shower. "That's what I said," she called over the sound of the water.

"But why? After all that happened? After he left with no explanation? After all these months of silence? I don't understand."

Stephanie didn't respond, but Laura didn't give in. She waited until her roommate stepped out of the shower and dried herself.

"So, tell me what's going on."

Stephanie pulled her peach-colored housecoat around her and busied herself looking through her closet. She wanted to find something to really knock his socks off. She certainly didn't want him thinking that she'd been sitting around pining for him all these months. She didn't want him to think that she had actually taken his proposal seriously, for Pete's sake. She didn't want him to have any idea that she was harboring a nest of butterflies in her stomach that would fill this room with fluttering color.

"Steph! Talk to me!"

Without looking around, she said, "There's nothing to talk about. He's one of our clients, that's all. He showed up at the office today, out of the blue, and invited me to dinner. I accepted. End of story."

"Did he tell you what was so all fired important that he had to cut his tour short?"

"Nope. I didn't ask, either. What difference does it make at this late date? All of that's history."

"But you were so upset, so hurt, so angry."

"And I managed to get over it."

Laura watched as Stephanie pulled out a midnight-blue dress with sheer sleeves and a plunging neckline. "You're not going to wear *that*, are you?" she asked in shocked surprise.

"What's wrong with it?"

"Nothing, if you're not worried about his blood pressure. My God! He'll think you're trying to seduce him!"

"Nonsense. I've worn this dress with Kent before. He never noticed."

"But that's Kent. He never notices anything," Laura muttered. "The man's wrapped up in his own little world."

Slipping the dress over her head, Stephanie replied, "Don't be silly. Kent's aware of everything that goes on around him."

Laura sighed. "I was afraid of that. So he's just been careful not to acknowledge the fact that he knows I'd give my eyeteeth to go out with him." She sank on the side of Stephanie's bed.

Stephanie jerked the dress down so that she could see. "Are you serious? You're interested in Kent? You've always been so flippant and sarcastic when he's around. I thought you didn't even like him."

"Yeah, well, what could I do? I thought you two were going to get married. Then you didn't. Then you continued to see each other and I haven't been certain what's been happening." She looked at her friend and grinned. "Don't get me wrong, now. I'm not suffering from pangs of unrequited love or anything. I just find the man appealing, that's all."

Stephanie began to laugh. "So why haven't you said something before now, you idiot?"

"And have you feel sorry for me? Nothing doing. Besides, if you're right, Kent probably already knows how I feel and is just being chivalrous and ignoring it."

"Believe me, Kent is not that chivalrous. He thinks the world of you and always has."

"You think so?"

"I know so." Stephanie shook her head in wonder. Sitting down in front of her mirror she began to briskly brush her hair. She would wear it down tonight. Maybe touch up the ends with the curling iron. She smiled, thinking of the way Alex had always seemed to love to run his hands through her hair.

Stop it! Didn't you learn your lesson last spring?

"My God, you're glowing! What are you thinking of? If it's Kent, I might as well forget him."

"I was just thinking about how nice it would be to see two close friends such as you and Kent manage to work out a relationship together, that's all." Stephanie prayed for forgiveness for the white lie. Although that wasn't what she had been thinking at the time, it was the truth. The next time she saw Kent she would have to mention Laura to him. Subtly, of course.

The doorbell rang and Stephanie looked at the clock.

"Would you mind getting the door, Laura? That should be Colonel Sloan."

She heard Laura's lighter tones, then Alex's deeper ones in the other room, and tried to calm down by taking a long, slow breath. She glanced at her hair in dismay. She didn't have time to do anything else to it. It had grown considerably since last spring. Should she wear it down or take the time to pull it back in its usual style?

She shook her head, watching it ripple around her shoulders. This would have to do. She quickly reached for her shoes, found the earrings she'd purchased to go with the dress, grabbed her purse and left the bedroom.

Alex had never seen her looking so beautiful. The dark blue dress accented her silver-blond hair as it fell into waves around her face and onto her shoulders. The dress had a deep V neck that drew his eyes to the rounded shape of her breasts, then narrowed into a small waistline and flared into folds that ended just below her knees. For a moment he couldn't say anything for the lump that had formed in his throat at the sight of her.

The first thing Stephanie saw when she stepped out of her room was the dazed expression on Laura's face. Not that she could blame her. Alex, as usual, looked absolutely smashing. He was wearing civilian clothing, and the subtle shades set off his dark good looks.

"Alex, I'd like you to meet my roommate, Laura. Laura, this is Colonel Sloan. You've heard me mention him a time or two," she said with a mischievous grin.

Alex extended his hand. "I'm really very pleased to meet you at last, Laura."

She held out her hand. "Me, too," Laura managed to say, "I mean, uh, yes."

Stephanie began to laugh. As long as she had known Laura she had never seen her quite so disconcerted.

Alex turned to Stephanie. "Are you ready to go?"

She nodded and turned to Laura. "I'll see you later."

Stephanie realized that her heart hadn't pounded this hard and this unevenly since the last time she'd been around this man. The Heart Association should use him as their national pinup.

Alex kept the conversation casual on the way to the restaurant, and Stephanie was willing to let him take the lead. She really had nothing to say to the man and couldn't understand what she was doing out with him, other than the fact she seemed to have no willpower where he was concerned.

It was only after they were seated in one of New York's finer restaurants and had given their order to the waiter that Alex reached over and took one of Stephanie's hands.

"I want to explain to you what happened last spring, Steph."

"I'm fully aware of what happened last spring. I don't need you to draw me any pictures."

"No. I mean about why I had to leave."

"You don't owe me any explanations, either. Not at this late date."

"I couldn't tell you then."

"And you don't need to tell me now."

"I want to."

"Why?"

"Because I want to get our relationship back on track."

"What relationship, Alex? We were on the road together, we became intimate. It's now over. There's nothing to discuss, and quite frankly, I find the whole episode embarrassing."

He studied her face in the soft light. "Why, because I left you? Or are you embarrassed because you acted upon your feelings rather than pretending that they didn't exist?"

"I don't see that it really matters at this point."

"There's something about me that I want you to know, regardless of what you decide about us—what we might have together." He glanced around the room, instinctively noticing who was nearby. There was no one. They had a secluded table. "The position I have at the Pentagon is a cover for what I actually do. Less than a handful of people know that. In addition to being part of the air force, I'm also in a special branch of intelligence. When there's a crisis somewhere, I'm generally the one who gets called out to check on it and decide what we can do."

From his expression anyone would think he was discussing the latest baseball scores. He picked up his glass of wine and sipped from it, never taking his eyes off her.

Stephanie felt as though she'd been slugged in the pit of her stomach with a doubled up fist. "That phone call?" she asked faintly.

"Yes. I'm never given a choice. If they call me, I know it's serious and I have to leave."

"And that night was one of those times?"

"Yes. I can't tell you where I went or what I did. But while I was away, I realized that I could no longer live that way, regardless of what I believed in and what I was hoping to accomplish." He absently turned his wineglass by its stem. "When I got back, I told them that I'd had enough. I want out."

"Out?"

"I've opted for retirement, Stephanie. I'm overdue. Too many things have happened that I can't change, no matter how hard I try. And I'm tired of losing everyone I hold dear to me."

Stephanie saw a muscle jerk in his cheek. Then he picked up his wineglass and took a long swallow. When he set the glass down, his eyes met hers once more. "Steve died while I was away," he said, his voice gruff with emotion.

"No! But I thought he was improving."

"They believe the strain was too much for his heart. They told me he went in his sleep, very peacefully. I don't know. I wasn't there."

Stephanie reached over and placed her hand on his. "I'm really sorry, Alex. I know what he meant to you."

He cleared his throat. "I had already made up my mind, but losing Steve was yet another sign. I don't want to lose anyone else. I found you, and I had to walk out on you without giving you any sort of explanation. That was the hardest thing I've ever had to do. I knew you were angry. You had every right to be, but there wasn't a thing I could do about it. Not then."

His gaze met hers. "Is there anything I can do now that would make any difference to you?"

Stephanie could feel herself trembling. So much had been said during these past few moments that changed how she had been viewing him, and viewing herself. It had never occurred to her that he was anywhere other than at his office in Washington during these last four months . . . only a phone call away.

Instead, he'd been God knows where under conditions she would never know.

And he'd lost Steve.

The waiter arrived with their meal, and as she watched him carefully set out what they had ordered, she remembered the night of the fire alarm scare in Seattle when Alex had sat there entertaining her with stories of him and Steve in order to get her mind off what was happening. That was the first time he had revealed who he was to her. That was the night she first realized that she was in love with the man.

And now he was asking her if there was anything he could do that would make a difference. .

"You just did," she murmured, when the waiter left them.

"I just did what?" he asked, puzzled.

"You gave me back my trust and belief in people... in you. It never occurred to me that you would have an explanation for leaving the tour other than the fact that the tour wasn't that important to you."

"To be honest, the tour wasn't nearly as important as you were. I had finally gotten you to say that you would accept a ring from me. Remember?"

She smiled. "Oh, yes. I remember. I thought I'd been a complete fool."

"And now?"

"I would be honored to wear your ring, Colonel Sloan. I love you very much."

His face lightened and his eyes grew brighter. He picked up his fork and began to eat, as though for the first time in a long time he was hungry.

"And you'll marry me?" he asked after a moment.

She nodded, too filled with emotion to speak.

"As soon as I'm relieved of my duties, there's no reason why I can't move to New York. You might get a little tired of me hanging around the house all day, though."

"What about your book?"

"There is that. My agent has been approached about my signing a three-book contract with the publisher of *Bridges to Burn*."

"Alex, that's wonderful."

He sat back and looked at her, a little surprised. "Yes, I guess it is, now that I think about it. I guess my mind's been on other things these last few months. Writing was the last thing I was thinking of."

Their main course was delivered and they began to eat. Stephanie kept glancing at Alex. Whenever she looked at him, she found him watching her with a smile on his face.

Finally, she could take no more of it. "What is it? Am I wearing dressing on my nose? What?"

He shook his head. "It's just so good to see you once more. I don't think I ever want to let you out of my sight again."

"You don't have to, you know. When do you have to go back to Washington?"

"I'm on official leave starting today, until October tenth. I didn't even take time to change. I hopped a commuter flight and came looking for you."

"So where are you staying?"

"I've got a hotel room in midtown Manhattan."

They gazed at each other, smiling. There was something about hotel rooms....

"Oh, Alex!" Stephanie suddenly remembered.

"What!"

"I'm leaving for Hawaii next week. It's been set up for months."

"No problem. I understand that Hawaii is a great place to spend a honeymoon."

... it was.

Epilogue

Stephanie glanced at her watch as she let herself into the apartment. It was only a little after two o'clock. Alex would be surprised to have her home so early. But she had some fantastic news for him.

She closed the door quietly, not wanting to disturb him if he was writing. He'd told her that morning that he had a new idea for a story that he was thinking about.

Not that he didn't deserve some time off. He'd written three books in the past five years, all bestsellers. The royalties had paid for their present surroundings that kept her close enough to work to be a real convenience.

Quietly walking down the hallway, she heard Alex talking, and wondered if he was on the phone. She peeked into his office but it was empty.

His voice was coming from the back of the apartment. She looked out on the terrace and saw him sitting in the lounge chair, holding their infant son, Steve, and talking to him.

She grinned and walked across the wide expanse of living room. "I don't know why I bothered to hire a baby-sitter. I thought you were going to work today."

Alex glanced up and saw her. He looked downright sheepish as he got out of his chair. "What are you doing home? I thought you intended to spend the day at the office, visiting with everyone."

"And where is Gladys?"

"I sent her home. I didn't feel like working anyway."

She shook her head, then put her arm around his neck and kissed him. "You're spoiling him rotten," she whispered, then looked at the four-month-old baby on his arm.

"No, I'm not. You get to play with him all the time. He's always asleep when I check on him."

"Was Gladys upset?"

"Why should she be? I paid her anyway."

"Alex!"

"Well, I didn't want to upset her, okay?" He sat down again, and patted the chair next to him. "Now, then. What are you doing home? You said Harry wanted you to come in for the day. He had some meetings he wanted you to sit in on. I take it he wants you to come back to work?"

"Something like that," she admitted, sitting down beside him.

"And what did you tell him?"

"That I'd have to check with you, first."

"Stephanie, what kind of nonsense is that? You know that I've never said anything about your working. You're the one who decided how long you'd work, when you got pregnant, and how long you intended to stay home."

"If you will remember correctly, I always talked it over with you first."

"I guess so."

"And I just thought I should discuss this with you."

Alex put the baby on his shoulder and began to stroke his back. "So what's to decide?"

"Well, I've been offered the opportunity to do a really fabulous tour—to Japan, Hong Kong, Taiwan, Australia, New Zealand. I'll be promoting this fantastically sexy celebrity. We'll be traveling together, just like any other tour. I'm the envy of every woman at Harry's office."

Alex's eyes darkened but he didn't say anything for a moment. Then in a deceptively casual tone he asked, "How long will the tour take?"

"Six weeks."

"Six weeks? Are you crazy? You'd leave me and Steve for six weeks while you go off with some guy that's probably used to having his way with every woman around?"

"Well, he does have a certain rather rakish reputation."

"And you'd even consider going on such a tour?"

"Like I said, I told Harry I'd talk with you, first."

"Fine. We just talked."

"And?"

"And . . . do what you want to do."

"You'll leave the choice up to me?"

He got up and walked into the apartment. Carrying the baby, he went down the hallway into the nursery that they had spent weeks getting ready and carefully placed Steve in the crib.

Stephanie watched from the doorway.

He took her hand and led her into the bedroom, over to the bed, then began to systematically undress her.

"Alex," she began to laugh, "what do you think you're doing?"

"I don't know. Whenever you start talking about going on six-week tours to exotic locales with sexy celebrities, I get nervous. And when I get nervous I find the most soothing thing I can do for my nerves is to make love to you." He started to grin as she quickly began to help him remove his own clothes.

"I see. Well, whatever we can do to relieve your stress sounds great to me."

He drew her down on the bed and began to kiss and caress her. She forgot all about their conversation until he finally drew away from her. "Are you really considering going on that tour?"

She slowly opened her eyes, trying to focus her mind on what he was saying. "Oh, yes. I've always wanted to see those places. But of course, if you don't want me to go . . ."

He kissed her again—slowly, with a great deal of feeling. "I just want you to be happy, love," he finally said, "whatever that takes."

"Fine," she murmured. "I'll let Harry know tomorrow that I'll take the assignment." She closed her eyes and began to kiss him across his chest.

He sighed. "Who is this guy who's going on the tour with you?"

"He's a very famous author whose books about the East have made quite an impact over there. His publisher said to spare no expense. But Harry didn't see any point in wasting money, so he decided to hire the celebrity's wife as his publicist, since that's how they met in the first place."

Alex grabbed her around the waist and pushed her away from him. "Are you talking about me?" he demanded.

"Umm-hmm."

"You wretch! You wanted me to believe that you were actually thinking about going off with some sexy celebrity for six weeks and—"

"That's exactly what I want to do. We can take Steve with us, and Gladys, and take some time off to see some of the sights as we go. I explained how you hate back-to-back appearances. Harry kept saying, 'Whatever it takes to make him happy.' I was also cautioned to try to keep you occupied so you wouldn't suddenly leave the tour in the middle again. I told him I'd do my best to keep you happy."

Alex shook his head and began to laugh. "I never know what you're going to do next, you know that?" he finally managed to say.

She leaned over him and whispered, "That's what a good publicist is for, love," and kissed him.

There were no more complaints in the Alexander Sloan family.

*   *   *   *   *

Silhouette Desire®

1989
IS THE YEAR
OF THE MAN!

What makes a romance? A special man, of course, and Silhouette Desire celebrates that fact with *twelve* of them! From Mr. January to Mr. December, every month spotlights the Silhouette Desire hero—our **MAN OF THE MONTH.**

Sexy, macho, charming, irritating…irresistible! Nothing can stop these men from sweeping you away. Created by some of your favorite authors, each man is custom-made for pleasure—*reading* pleasure—so don't miss a single one.

Diana Palmer kicks off the new year, and you can look forward to magnificent men from **Joan Hohl, Jennifer Greene** and many, many more. So get out there and find your man!

Silhouette Desire's

MAN OF THE MONTH . . .

MAND-1

ATTRACTIVE, SPACE SAVING BOOK RACK

Display your most prized novels on this handsome and sturdy book rack. The hand-rubbed walnut finish will blend into your library decor with quiet elegance, providing a practical organizer for your favorite hard-or soft-covered books.

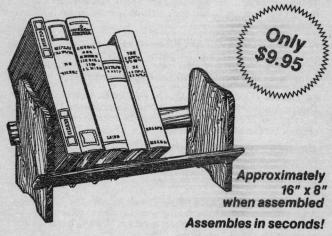

Only $9.95

Approximately 16" x 8" when assembled

Assembles in seconds!

To order, rush your name, address and zip code, along with a check or money order for $10.70* ($9.95 plus 75¢ postage and handling) payable to *Silhouette Books*.

Silhouette Books
Book Rack Offer
901 Fuhrmann Blvd.
P.O. Box 1396
Buffalo, NY 14269-1396

Offer not available in Canada.

BKR-2A

*New York and Iowa residents add appropriate sales tax.

 # Silhouette Desire

COMING NEXT MONTH

#469 RELUCTANT FATHER—Diana Palmer
Meet our JANUARY MAN-OF-THE-MONTH, Blake Donavan.
Tough. Formidable. He lived alone and liked it that way. His
nemesis was love, but he had one obsession—her name was
Meredith Calhoun.

#470 MONTANA'S TREASURES—Janet Bieber
G.T. Maddox loved his land too much to let Amanda Lukenas
destroy it. He figured he'd offer some old-fashioned hospitality
featuring his own special brand of...friendly persuasion.

#471 THAT FONTAINE WOMAN!—Helen R. Myers
District Attorney Adam Rhodes didn't like Fontaines and Diana was
no exception. She was the kind of woman he knew he could never
control, but one he ached to possess.

#472 HEARTLAND—Sherryl Woods
Friends. Steven Drake and Lara Danvers had once been much more
than that. Now Steven had come back and he wanted Lara *and* her
farm. Could she trust him...this time?

#473 TWILIGHT OVER EDEN—Nicole Monet
Amber Stevenson had to betray the man she loved to protect him
from scandal and disgrace. She still loved Joe Morrow, but the secrets
remained along with her passion.

#474 THIN ICE—Dixie Browning
Maggie Duncan had left a high-powered job and a failed marriage for
her grandfather's cabin. She'd found peace in her solitude—but that
was before Sam Canady arrived!

AVAILABLE NOW: